Howling Storm

Magic of Nasci Book 8

by

DM FIKE

Avalon Labs LLC

For Thomas, who believes my stories could be movies.

CHAPTER 1

I HATE IT when urban legends turn out to be true. Especially when I have to take care of it.

Normally, I don't take house calls. Yet there I was, standing on the back porch of a house built into a hillside. This porch led into a dingy basement, the sliding glass doors the only source of natural light for the whole floor. The top floor above me had a nice wide balcony facing Siltcoos Lake, which would have increased the value of the house if the owner had kept up with routine maintenance. Faded green housepaint, one slightly rotting beam, and the knee-high dandelions in the lawn, though, weighed down its potential max value.

"You sure this is a paying customer?" I asked the pensive plumber next to me. Oscar Soto generally wore a smile with his black-framed glasses, work shirt, and overalls, so the fact he couldn't be bothered now put another strike against this dubious job. He more resembled his game warden cousin with a frown and furrowed eyebrows under jet black hair.

Oscar nodded. "Mrs. Welch always pays. Just might take a week or two since it's generally by check, and she only goes to the post office on Mondays."

"I'm not waiting for snail mail to get paid," I said. "I'll need cash immediately after I'm done."

"Of course."

Oscar may have been the trained professional, but we both had something better than being officially licensed and bonded. Oscar and I possessed ken, the ability to recognize the goddess Nasci's elemental wonders in the world around us. For Oscar, that meant he could "sense" water flowing through pipes, a very handy ability for someone who installed sinks and fixed toilets.

I, however, was a full-blown shepherd of the goddess who lived in the center of our planet, her energy sustaining all life as we know it. Not only could I sense a clogged pipe, I was attuned to earth, air, and fire as well. I could manipulate those elements by writing sacred sigils and directing Nasci's will through my own magical pithways. It was my sworn duty to hone that power to battle evil beasts from a parallel universe that constantly threatened to devour the animals of our world.

Oscar knew none of this, seeing me only as someone with helpful abilities superior to his own. I only accepted his jobs because I had a cash flow problem, and he offered me a way to solve it with minimal effort. This was the third job I'd done for him in so many weeks, and after a debacle getting paid the first time, he'd gotten used to paying me immediately.

I stepped toward the house. "What are we working on today?"

"Not we," Oscar replied, not moving behind me. "You."

I swung my head to give him my hairy eyeball. "Say what now?"

Oscar folded his arms over his chest. "I ain't going in until you get rid of the snake first."

My brain ground to a halt. "What?"

Oscar's cheeks reddened, but he held his stubborn stance. "Vincent said you're good with animals."

Wonderful. I doubted my sorta boyfriend had told Oscar the whole truth about nature wizards, but then again, who knew what came up during one of their family's infamous Sunday lunches? I'd shown up once, gotten accused of being morally loose with my body, and ended up dumping iced tea all over Vincent's mother.

Fun times.

"Oscar, start at the beginning. What do snakes have to do with you calling me in for a plumbing job?"

I pieced it together with a few more prodding questions. As it turned out, Oscar hated snakes. A common enough phobia, but one made especially difficult when you entered a flooded bathroom with a kingsnake swimming around. Oscar had noticed the reptile and noped it right out of there, deciding I could handle it.

Suddenly, Oscar's all caps text this morning made a lot of sense. "Let's summarize, shall we? You got called into a job on a derelict house, discovered the bottom floor flooded, and decided you should call a five-foot tall woman in as animal control because you can't handle a single snake. That sound about right?"

"You make me look bad when you put it that way," Oscar complained, although he had a twinkle in his eye. "But yes."

I rubbed a hand across my now throbbing forehead. "What have I done to deserve this?"

"You're tough," Oscar said, channeling his inner high school coach. "You can do this."

I glared at him through my fingers. "I want double my fee."

"Done," he replied without hesitation.

Wow. I didn't actually think that would work. Oscar must have really hated snakes. Maybe I should have asked for more.

"Fair warning, I won't kill the snake. I'm releasing him back into the wild."

"Cool. Cool." He shoved an industrial flashlight into

my hand. "Take your time. The bathroom's the only open doorway to the back. Come get me when you're done." Then Oscar made a hasty retreat to his white van parked in the gravel driveway up the hill. Coward.

Well, it was time to put up or shut up. I rolled up my hoodie sleeves and slid open the glass doors.

The oh-so-pleasant smell of organic rot assailed me as I crossed the threshold into a dark living room. Glancing over my shoulder and confirming no one else could see me, I gathered air pith into my palms and drew two infinity symbols in the air. A cocoon of swirling air immediately shielded my head. I normally only use this sigil because I can't breathe, but the smell was so bad that I needed some sort of filtration to clear the air around me.

I flicked on the flashlight instead of using a fingerflame to conserve energy. A narrow beam of light uncovered the even darker room toward the back. The old shag carpet squished deep, wet fabric tendrils curling around my boots. Ew, both for the outdated rug and the water damage. I hoped after this fiasco the homeowner would consider some serious upgrades.

Once inside the bathroom, standing in a thin puddle, I swung the light around the room. I intended to catch sight of the snake. And I did find him, plus a whole lot more.

"Yikes."

It wasn't just one snake, but an entire clutch worth of babies. Their stripes writhed on every surface: around the toilet, over the lip of the tub, and even up the pedestal sink. I counted nine spaghetti noodle bodies in the near dark, although it was next to impossible to conduct an accurate census since they wiggled around so fast. I had no idea how I was supposed to wrangle them all out.

"Definitely should have asked for triple," I groaned.

Well, you have to start somewhere, so I began with a vague appeal. Animals understand shepherds exist to protect them. They'll often listen to our commands. In my best fake cheerful voice, I called out, "Hey, guys! Party's over. Why don't I show you the way out?"

This caught the attention of two of the smaller snakes next to me. I kept up a light chatter and backed away from the door, grateful when they both followed me. Within a few minutes, I had them winding through shag carpet like fake grass, then outside and across the derelict lawn. They wandered happily out of sight into the trees.

With a working game plan, I repeated the process. It took more coaxing to get a third one out, but she eventually dragged her scales like a kid being told to leave a playground.

The other six (seven?) had no interest in listening to Big Mama shepherd. They continued to splash around the tiles, completely ignoring my closing calls.

I considered bribing them out with a tasty treat, but snakes eat other living animals. While followers of Nasci are okay with the circle of life, we also vow to protect that circle, not exploit it. It felt wrong to kill a bird or rodent just because I was strapped for cash, so I quickly gave up that idea.

That left manual extraction. I stepped inside the bathroom, ignoring my disgust at water splashing over my laces near the toilet. Thankful that shepherds don't generally get infections, I reached around the sink and pulled a snake out from behind the base. The snake hissed and twisted for an instinctual bite, but I got my other hand wrapped behind his head before he could strike. Not a small feat, given how small and slippery he was.

"You'll be happier in the forest," I told him firmly as I marched him outside. I was going to leave him on the lawn, but he tried to follow me back inside, so I had to pick him up again and deposit him farther into the woods.

I got a second one out the same way, but the third managed to bite my thumb pretty hard. Resisting the urge to squeeze the offender in half, I ignored my throbbing hand until I released her back into the wild. Kingsnakes aren't poisonous even to vanilla humans, but it's never fun to be dual-punctured like a stapler.

Wishing I could draw some sigils to speed things up, I assessed the placement of Oscar's van. He'd backed the vehicle up to the house, the driver's seat completely out of view. Without windows in the back of the van, he could only see out the sideview mirror. I couldn't see his reflection no matter what angle I walked around the yard.

Satisfied I could cast more magic in secret, I changed tactics. Since the remaining visible snakes were all curled inside puddles, it was simply a matter of drawing a water sigil to lift both snake and water into the air to scoop them up. I used these magic bubbles to safely remove three more snakes.

After I gently laid the last snake into a pile of fallen autumn leaves, I sighed in relief. "That wasn't so bad," I mentally patted myself on the shoulder. I almost went up to tell Oscar I'd finished but decided to check the bathroom one last time to make sure I'd caught them all.

I should have let it go, or at least not cursed myself with my last spoken words.

There was one final baby kingsnake left in the bathroom. I'd missed her because I hadn't checked inside the bathtub thoroughly. Only the very tip of her triangle head appeared out of the dark waters. At a glance, she only appeared a few inches long, which was not possible. Squinting, I pointed the flashlight straight down to find the rest of her body.

That's when I realized she was halfway inside the tub's drain.

I stared into her beady black eyes. "Time to join your brothers and sisters. C'mon."

She flicked her tongue at me.

I interpreted that as a serpentine middle finger. Scowling, I gathered more water pith into my palm. "It wasn't a request. You're coming whether you like it or not."

I drew the same water sigil, but it didn't work like the

three snakes before. Waves swirled around her face, and I pulled up a watery globe, but she remained firmly anchored in the drain. I couldn't sense a lot of water pith in the drain itself, so either the pipe was clogged or she'd wedged her scales in so tightly, I couldn't lift her.

She bared her fangs at me.

"Stubborn little snake," I hissed right back at her. I tentatively put a hand in the water at the edge of the tub where she couldn't reach me. It was hard to sense any moving pith underneath the porcelain, but I wanted to locate any water flowing in the pipes around the drain. Maybe I couldn't lift her out with water, but I could try blasting her out.

When I felt a faint current somewhere in the general vicinity, I tested to see if it was connected to the drain by moving it up the pipe. The kingsnake flailed violently as the water pushed up against her.

I smiled. Gotcha.

"I'll give you one last chance to come out on your own," I told her solemnly.

She displayed more of the inside of her mouth.

"Fine. Suit yourself."

Honestly, I should just give up being smug. Whenever I am, it's almost always a prelude to something disastrous, and unfortunately, my brilliant plan to water cannon the snake out of the drain was no exception. Because as it turned out, jerking the current back up the pipe only exacerbated the leak that had caused the mess in the first place.

So yes, I dislodged the snake, along with gallons and gallons of squirting water right in my face. I fell backward, landing butt first and chest deep in wastewater. I did manage to catch the snake. Or rather, she caught me as she bit down on my earlobe as she flew past.

My pride may have been drenched, and I earned an accidental ear piercing, but at least I cleared up one myth: snakes can indeed travel up household drains under the right circumstances.

CHAPTER 2

OSCAR LATER THEORIZED that a pregnant kingsnake must have made a late nest of eggs under the house. Whether the nest caused or merely exacerbated the burst pipe is not clear, but it ended up so large a job, he eventually had to call in some buddies to help him patch everything up.

In the immediate aftermath of The Incident, however, I should have won an award for my self-control because I didn't bury Oscar under bedrock. He laughed at my appearance. His scaredy-snake ass apparently thought I looked hilarious drenched from head to toe. Only when his guffaws hit the minute mark did I realize I could have drawn a drying sigil before he saw me and saved myself the humiliation. My only defense is that I'd been too disgruntled to think straight. Oscar only had the decency to appear a little sheepish when I pointed out the cut to my earlobe, but it had stopped bleeding by then and probably didn't look all that bad.

"We will never speak of this again." I snatched the cash out of his hands and shoved it in my hoodie pouch, the moisture ensuring it would not fall out anytime soon.

As he wiped the tears away, he asked, "Not even to

Vincent?"

I stiffened. It was exactly because I'd done a job for Oscar without telling Vincent that we weren't on good speaking terms. "Tell him anything you want. I won't be accused of hiding things from him again."

That finally sobered Oscar up. "I'm sorry if things between you are strained."

"I'm sure you are," I said sarcastically. When he reddened, I sighed. "Look, if you really want to help, I was going to send him a text to tell him what we've been up to. A picture might be worth a thousand words in this case. You up for a selfie with me?"

Oscar grinned. "If anything can get through his recent bad attitude, you drenched from rescuing snakes oughta do it."

He leaned into my shoulder as I held my phone as far from our faces as I could. I refrained from smiling so as not to ruin the effect of my soaked clothes. In contrast, Oscar flashed the camera the peace sign. Appraising the picture, we were a study in idiot opposites, which was exactly what I was going for.

After sending the pic off to Vincent with a short description of the job, I asked, "So Vince's pouting even with you guys, huh?"

"Yeah, he's got a little black cloud over him. He won't talk to me about it. I think he misses you."

I tapped the phone to my forehead. "He could text me back, but he doesn't seem interested."

Oscar scowled. "I love my cousin, man, but he can be so stupid sometimes. Just because his mom made a scene doesn't mean he should be punishing you. You're by far and away the nicest person he's ever dated."

I beamed. "Well, that's nice."

Oscar slid on a sly smile. "It's not a big club. Only you and his ex-wife."

My pride fell right back to its original starting position. "Gee thanks for the huge compliment." I thought of the pretty brunette who was Vincent's high school sweetheart and friend of his family. "Still, at least I beat out Christy."

"It's not tough competition," he said dryly. "You talked to her at Tita's house, remember? She's always that charming."

She had been rather rude to me, but then again, I elicited that kind of response from a lot of people. "I thought your families were all buddy-buddy."

"Our parents are, but we have our own relationships with each other. Christy and I never got along, but maybe that had something to do with the frog I stuck in her backpack in the third grade."

"Ooh, that's mean. Funny, but mean." Then I tilted my head. "So, you're okay picking up frogs, but not snakes?"

"I don't trust anything that moves by squirming itself around. It ain't natural."

"Spoken like a guy who messes with sewer lines for a living." I was getting tired of standing around in wet boots. I needed to find a place to magically dry myself off before I accidentally used my real abilities in front of Oscar.

"I got to get going." I waved vaguely at the house. "Good luck with all that."

"Thanks again. And Ina," he called as I walked back toward the lake's small public access lot where I'd lied and said I'd parked "my car." "Don't worry about Vincent. He'll come around."

I decided not to jinx that prediction with words as I slipped over the hill, drawing drying sigils once out of sight.

* * *

I walked at a leisurely pace through dense Douglas firs and cedars, stepping around ferns and late blooming wildflowers. Normally I would have enjoyed the quiet stroll through wisp channels to Sipho's homestead, but today my bad mood interfered. Vincent's radio silence really did gnaw at me. I missed him terribly. My hormone-driven body yearned to cuddle up against him on his worn futon. But even romantic feelings aside, he had become my best friend, someone I could say anything to without fear of judgment or retribution. Not having him available to talk to was taking its toll.

The southern Talol Wilds shepherds were at a critical juncture. We'd lost Tabitha, one of our two powerful augurs, and although we'd recently upgraded an incredibly talented fire shepherd to take her place, whispers from the north threatened to take away our autonomy. We were deemed too unstable, too weak to keep operating independently from the more bureaucratic northern homestead.

Darby, Tabitha's former eyas and now full-blown shepherd, had already begun the process of changing her alliance. She blamed me for Tabitha's death and wanted to get as far away from me as possible. She also petitioned to take her Columbia Gorge territory with her. The northern homestead already covered over 60% of the Talol Wilds with Washington state, northern Idaho, and western British Columbia. Taking over a huge swatch of our border with the Columbia River would shrink our meager Oregon and northern California territory even further. If Darby succeeded, we could lose enough land and manpower to justify a joining of the two groups.

If the two homesteads merged into one, I was pretty sure I'd get demoted to the worst grunt work possible. I spoke my mind, didn't follow rules, and had unorthodox lightning magic to boot. And that was the best-case scenario. Sertalis, the head augur of the north, had already tried once to get me bound for good. I had no doubt he'd try something similar again if I were directly under his command.

To make matters even worse, we had a serious security problem in the south. A bound shepherd by the name of Rafe had created deep unnatural crevasses straight through to Nasci's lifeblood, what ordinary people know as magma. Although we'd defeated him, those fissures remained. We called them lesions, deep wounds that leaked Nasci's energy despite our best efforts to seal them. Vaetturs, the evil monsters that came to feed on our world from another dimension, had recently discovered these ripe feeding grounds, and those that had managed to absorb magma had grown almost too powerful to banish back to their worlds. Our forger Sipho had an idea how to seal the lesions, but it took her time and materials, both expensive commodities. That's why I'd taken Oscar's snake job: to earn money for more of Sipho's supplies. I intended to hit a hardware store on my way back.

But first, I figured I'd check in on the three lesions to make sure everything was okay. We had a rotation of shepherds guarding them constantly, but after fighting off a stallion-sized scorpion and a swarm of evil locusts in the past few weeks, it felt prudent to double-check.

I first stopped by the lesions near Whitaker Creek and Noti, located within twenty miles of each other. I noticed both shepherds guarding them, but kept my silence in the foliage, not wanting to get drawn into a conversation with either. Zibel—the earth shepherd with his freckled skin, red hair, and shifty eyes—didn't like me much to begin with. Slender and pale air shepherd Euchloe didn't have anything against me per se, but I could only take so much of her New Age propaganda before my mind melted out of my ears. I confirmed nothing creepy lurked in the shadows. The only abnormality was the higher-than-usual number of black-tailed deer.

The deer got out of hand as I approached the last leaking lesion near McGowan Creek, inside the more central forests of Oregon. I kept seeing them in my peripheral vision, blending into the vertical lines of trunks, some adorned with branch-like antlers. None of them grazed or moved like normal animals, but simply watched me as silent sentries. I called out to several, but they merely blinked and drifted off a few feet. I'd grown used to the black-tailed deer's presence near lesions. They were as attracted to the lesions as vaetturs. Still, something about their behavior put me on edge.

I approached the gully surrounding the final lesion. Autumn now reigned over all the deciduous trees, their bright yellows and oranges contrasting with the more somber tones of the stubborn evergreens. Leafless branches revealed a partly cloudy sky. Hiking over the ridge, I found the small stream marking the unnatural crevasse. Brush and grass refused to grow near the bare patch of dirt.

Even worse, no shepherd stood guard. I put my hands over my mouth, intending to yell out a name, but I couldn't recall who specifically had been assigned to watch over this lesion.

My hesitation cost years of my lifespan as a sudden voice boomed overhead, scaring me so badly I fell to my knees.

"Good afternoon, Ina!"

Already on the ground, I glanced up into a nearby ponderosa pine. A third of the way from the top-most bough sat a Paul Bunyan of a man, complete with bushy black beard and eyebrows. This lumberjack had traded his overalls for a shredded organic cloak, his hairy feet bare.

Guntram, the augur who trained me and air master extraordinaire.

"Why are you roosting up there like one of your kidama?"

He stretched his arms out wide as if he'd just woken up. "I'm recycling my air pith. It helps pass the time." Then, he drew a wind gust sigil and floated gracefully down to me.

"Yeah, well, you about gave me a heart attack," I muttered, envious of his casual air usage.

"Why are you here? No one is scheduled to take over my position until after sunset."

"I didn't mean to startle you. I actually meant to sneak a peek and be on my way." I realized something else was off about this particular encounter. "And where are your ravens anyway? They should have warned me a mile away that you'd be on duty."

"They're scattered across both the Willamette and Siuslaw forests, scouting for vaetturs. Collectively they are better able to spot one than our meager numbers."

All augurs have a group of animals that they can communicate with telepathically. Kidama are kind of like species-specific minions, although the relationship is a bit more symbiotic than master and pet. Thinking of Guntram's ravens roaming across the forests reminded me of Tabitha's former kidama.

"Your ravens aren't the only eyes out there," I said to Guntram. "I'm sure you've noticed the black-tailed deer."

"Yes."

I waited for Guntram to say more, but he didn't appear willing to go past that one syllable. In fact, he crossed his arms over his chest, a sure sign that he felt he'd said enough on the subject.

His posture had never stopped me from asking questions as an eyas. It definitely didn't affect me now. "It's weird and you know it. Why are they hanging around?"

"I have my own theory."

Another wall of silence. "Which is…?"

"It's not anything proven, not by a long stretch."

"I'm listening."

"You should not go blabbing it around as some sort of truth."

I threw up my hands in exasperation. "I'm going to be eligible for senior citizen discounts at this rate. Spill it, Guntram."

He glared for a long moment but finally relented. "Tabitha lost her life to the magma. It is an unprecedented way for a shepherd to die. We were unable to retrieve her physical remains and return her properly to Nasci."

Followers of Nasci had strict rituals. I'd attended a dryant funeral once, where the body had been reabsorbed into the earth through a complex series of sigils. The corpse had melted away and new, beautiful vegetation sprung from the spot. Supposedly Nasci reclaimed that energy to be recycled and renewed again. (Cue songs about the circle of life.)

"Tabitha died inside magma. Isn't that basically the same thing as returning back to Nasci?"

"That's what we all assumed, but then your dreams of her gave me pause. Those happened as part of your Shepherd Trial, though, so I wrote them off as being unrelated. Once you passed your trial and you quit mentioning Tabitha to me, I assumed all to be well."

I knew where he was going. "But then Darby accidentally absorbed lesion energy when we fought the bundun and also had a vision of Tabitha. That's why she didn't pursue her petition to have me bound."

"And perhaps we could even explain that away as part of your Shepherd Trial." Guntram grimaced. "Nothing with you has ever been routine or easy."

I shrugged. "Hey, you took me on as an eyas. You didn't have to do that."

"But I did," Guntram said quietly. "Based on my own visions about you."

Well, that was new info to me. "You dreamed about me?"

Guntram nodded. "I had serious reservations taking you on as an eyas. You were…untraditional. And my observations of you interacting with the dryants showed you to be abrasive and impulsive."

While I was glad Guntram had outright avoided calling me a haggard, a derogatory term for shepherds trained after puberty, I didn't appreciate the less-than-flattering description of his first impression of me. "Sorry if I didn't act like a fairytale princess, singing to the woodland creatures all around me."

Guntram frowned. "You tried to ride Giles."

I cringed. "You saw that?"

Guntram nodded in full disapproval.

Giles is the mountain goat dryant who hangs around Mt. Jefferson. Like shepherds, dryants are animal spirits blessed with Nasci's magical gifts. They generally keep vaetturs off our backs, and we protect them as allies against creatures of Letum. Giles had come to check me out during a hike when my ken started manifesting itself. Standing eight feet tall with massive front shoulder blades and double-spiraled horns like corkscrews, he looked like the stuff of nightmares.

And I'd been so excited to meet another obviously magical creature, I'd tried to ride him. The only thing that stopped me was the thundering earthquake he produced at his hooves when I swung up for a mount.

I blushed but waved off my embarrassment. "Giles took care of himself. Nobody's gonna ride him that he doesn't want on his back."

Guntram huffed into his beard. "I did not see your recklessness as a positive trait, and yet, I felt a distinct pull to take you under my wing. It was only after much meditation and numerous dreams that I finally gave into those instincts."

"Does Nasci usually tell us stuff in dreams?"

"It depends on who you ask. Some shepherds seem more attuned to dream-based visions. Others never experience it. They often dismiss such things as wishful thinking. The northern homestead"—he scowled at the mention—"believes them to be completely unreliable."

"I could care less about those guys," I said. "Back to Tabitha's kidama. If your theory is true, then Tabitha's soul is essentially stuck. We have to help her somehow, don't we?"

Guntram nodded. "I discussed this at length with the Oracle. The best thing we can do is seal the lesions. Once

Nasci's wounds heal, theoretically the goddess will be able to properly absorb Tabitha, and her spirit should be able to pass on."

We couldn't leave a shepherd of Nasci in limbo. The stakes for sealing the lesions just rose a significant notch. I patted my kangaroo pouch. "I'm off to buy supplies for Sipho. You need me to relay anything back to the guys at the homestead?"

Guntram shook his head. "They're working as best as they can. All we can do is wait and watch."

Wait and watch, I thought as I left Guntram to his post. Ugh. Irrationally, I wished there was some sort of monster I could attack. It would be much better than this awful passage of time, where we had to be on our guard, never knowing what to expect.

CHAPTER 3

THE LAST TIME I'd visited the sprawling home improvement store in Springfield, I'd brought Sipho along. She'd driven me bonkers wandering through the aisles like Alice in Wonderland, only I couldn't blame her twitchy actions on recreational drug use. I'd since convinced Sipho I should go shopping without her. She only really agreed because she and her apprentice Callum had been busy making wards out of tungsten-based circular saws. Flying solo, I hoped this trip would be less dramatic.

Famous last words.

The front greeter waved to me, and then no one paid me any mind as I navigated the maze of tall shelves. I couldn't remember exactly where the circular saws were. I'd passed the plumbing supplies for the third time when a voice accompanied by a telltale hack drifted down the aisle.

"Ina, is that you?"

An older man wore overalls over a belly that made him look pregnant with a basketball. Next to his cart stood a similarly aged woman with polyester pants and ill-fitting floral blouse. She waved me to come closer.

"It's so good to see you!"

Carol and Dennis. They owned the aging gas station

19

and convenience store near Sipho's homestead. I used to go there for pop and snacks until Darby had attacked me with magic in the parking lot. Carol had witnessed the whole thing through the dirty glass door. I didn't dare show my face since my cover had been blown, and I certainly hadn't expected to run into them here. Although it made sense they had to come to Springfield now and again for "big city" supplies given their rural location.

I could have bolted, but that would only make things more awkward if they caught me shopping in another section of the store. I swallowed the saliva in my mouth and said, "Hi."

Carol trotted over to me, quite spry for someone so stocky. "Where have you been? I was just telling Dennis the other day we haven't seen you in weeks, maybe a few months."

I tried to keep the question out of my voice and failed. "I've been busy?"

Dennis grunted. "I told you, woman, you scared the poor girl off. She's fidgeting like a jackrabbit."

Carol's face flushed. "I had a cold."

"And you should have sucked it up." He pointed at me with one stubby finger. "What did she do to you?"

"Uh…" My mind stalled while trying to understand what was going on.

"You know what Carol told me after the last time you came to the store?" Dennis asked. "She called in a panic saying there was a weird fog, then earthquakes, and finally a lightning storm right outside the window. Then she claimed you convinced a bunch of deer to haul some blond girl off into the woods."

Yep, that accurately described my little run-in with Darby. I raised my hands in self-defense. "Well, I—"

But Carol cut me off. "I always get a little loopy when I take cold meds. I am so sorry if I said or did anything strange."

"She won't be taking them again, especially not when

manning the store," Dennis added.

I stared at them, mouth agape. Did they both really think she'd imagined the whole thing?

Carol patted me on the shoulder. "I feel so terrible. Say you'll come back to the store later? Free pop on us."

"Hey," Dennis protested.

"It's the least I can do for scaring the poor girl out of her wits. Just look at her. She's speechless."

I really was. I'd missed Carol and Dennis (and the easy access to bad food), but I'd dismissed the whole thing as a loss. Despite karma mostly gunning for my misery, it tossed me this one bone.

And I wasn't going to ignore it. "I'll take one free pop and then buy anything else myself. How does that sound?"

Carol beamed. "Of course."

Dennis grumbled something, but I'd known him long enough to recognize his satisfaction with my plan.

I couldn't help but smile. "I really ought to get going, but it was nice seeing you. Especially since we could clear things up."

"Our pleasure, dear," Carol said.

I started to walk away, but then paused. "You don't happen to know where the circular saws are, do you?"

Dennis raised an eyebrow. "First you buy me out of batteries and now you need tools. You taking up woodshop or something?"

"Something," I confirmed.

"Such a weird kid." He shook his head but added, "Go around the corner and down toward the back of the store. Take a right at the big screwdriver display. You can't miss it."

"Thanks. Catch you around."

I couldn't erase the goofy grin plastered on my face, which garnered strange looks from a construction crew I passed. He could deal with it. Against all odds, Darby hadn't ruined this special treat for me.

I should have gone straight back to Sipho's, but after the first wisp channel, I got distracted by a buzzing in my pocket. I pulled out my phone to find a text from one Vincent Garcia, responding to my earlier selfie with Oscar.

He'd written back simply, "Really?"

I placed the heavy paper bag with the circular saws on a dry rock as I contemplated my response. On one hand, the fact Vincent had written back at all was a good sign. On the other hand, I would have preferred more than a one-word response. Meanings are so difficult to convey in words. Was he irritated at me taking Oscar's job? Frustrated at my honesty? Laughing at how drenched I was?

Only one way to find out. I took a deep breath and wrote, "You up to chat?"

A painful minute went by. The last time I'd asked this question, Vincent had made a vague excuse on why he was busy. If he did it again, I had to decide how much more of this teenage crap I was going to put up with before I stopped trying.

Then those three nerve-wracking dots appeared as he wrote a response. They lingered way too long. He was either drafting a novel or rewriting his response over and over again.

It turned out to be the latter. "Better to talk in person. You free?"

My fingers flew without hesitation. "Yes."

He provided the name of a beach. "I'll be there in a half hour."

"Okay," I responded.

I couldn't lug the heavy metal tools with me, so I found a cavity in the base of a cedar near the wisp channel. After pushing my purchases inside and covering the bag with sticks to camouflage it, I dashed toward my destination.

One quirk of wisp channels is that sometimes it can

take you less time to travel a longer distance than a shorter one. The portals are fixed, and you have to hike between them. In this case, even though Sipho's homestead was only twenty-five miles away from where I started, it would have taken me at least that many minutes to make it home. I traveled nearly double that distance in half the time using a different route.

I arrived at the beach with the sun beginning its spectacular descent into the Pacific Ocean, a bright red disc tossing its luminosity onto rolling waves. A cold biting wind whipped black strands of hair that had gotten loose from my ponytail. Shivering despite having come into the sun, I drew a heat sigil for warmth. Vincent would have to trek over sand dunes to get here. Given the season, time of day, and remote location of the nearest road, he had picked the perfect location that ensured our privacy.

"Arf! Arf!"

A seal's bark broke my concentration. I raised my hand over my eyes so I could view past the glare into the ocean. Two knobby antlers attached to a triangular head floated toward me in the froth. The oversized harbor seal plopped itself on shore not far from me, wibbling around since its torpedo-shaped body was not built well for land. With bright blue streaks woven around his spine as if a seamstress had stitched them there, no one in their right mind would have mistaken him for a regular pinniped.

Not that a normal person could see him at all.

"Hey, Ronan!" I waded into the surf to meet him. "How's it going?"

Ronan barked in response, nudging his stiff bristle-like whiskers into my calves. Seals really are puppies of the sea, even when they are dryants. I scratched him affectionately between the antlers, happy high-pitched noises curling out of his throat.

"You like that, huh?" I hadn't seen much of Ronan since I saved him from a petrifying vaettur last spring. Our resident water shepherd, Baot, generally looked after the ocean dwellers. Unfortunately, Baot had temporarily abandoned his underwater post to help guard the lesions.

"You missing Baot?" I asked Ronan.

He growled. When I pulled away, he nipped at my hand to get me to continue petting him.

I took that as a yes. I plopped butt first in the waves, knowing I could dry myself off after Ronan had gotten his fill of me. The dryant bounced around me, drawing the attention of members of his pod. Seal noses poked out of the crests to stare at us, a few even plopping on shore next to us for a few affectionate pats (though Ronan made it clear to the others with snapping teeth that he'd reserved my affection first).

A laugh escaped my throat as blubbery bodies surrounded me. Honestly, I needed the love as much as they did. It had been a rough year. Reconnecting to the reason I'd become a shepherd in the first place—to protect Nasci's sacred creatures—reminded me that all the sleepless nights, sweat, and tears had been worth it.

The seals sensed the intruder before I did. Several young adults at the edge of the crowd launched themselves back into the water, giving out a cry of warning. The other seals followed as a voice called out to us.

"Hey!"

Ronan arched his head to bark at Vincent approaching us from the sand dunes. Vincent halted in his tracks as the two stared at each other. After one final head butt into my arm, Ronan dove off after the others, disappearing soundlessly beneath lapping waves.

Vincent stared at the spot where Ronan had vanished as I stood and drew a drying sigil for my wet boots. My lips upturned at the corners. "Never seen a seal with blue streaks and antlers before?"

Shaking his head, Vincent walked down toward me. "I'm sure it was just a trick of the light."

Vincent had major denial issues when it came to his ken. Even after he'd saved me once by halting a vaettur in his tracks (a trick that I still didn't understand how he'd pulled off), he didn't acknowledge that he had any magical powers. He'd grown up at odds with his family, many of whom claimed to have minor pith abilities. Oscar could sense water pith. And only people with ken could perceive vaetturs and dryants.

I raised an eyebrow at Vincent. "Do you really want to start our conversation with a lie?"

Vincent frowned. "No, I don't, but I have a feeling you won't let it go."

"You're right, I won't. This is the actually the third time you've met Ronan. The first two times, you couldn't see him even though he was sitting right in front of you."

"I didn't see him because he doesn't exist," Vincent snapped back.

"And what about the purple-feathered owl?" I asked. Vincent had admitted to spotting another dryant, Sova, before he'd gotten all huffy. I couldn't wait to hear how he'd deny that one.

"I must have been mistaken. It happens."

"You didn't think it was some weird trick before!" I fought to bring my voice back down. "What changed between then and now?"

Instead of a heated response, I got a sad sigh. "Lots of things have changed." It was only then did I notice the circles underneath his eyes.

"Are you not sleeping?"

"No, I'm not. We have a wolf issue up in Washington."

Vincent was a game warden for the state of Oregon, a position that straddled the line between state police officer and park ranger. He certainly didn't have jurisdiction in the state north of us. "What does that have to do with you?"

Vincent's gaze pierced me. "It killed Christy's uncle."

A gasp escaped my lips. Gray wolves had been reintroduced to Yellowstone and Idaho around the time I was born. Animals don't exactly recognize human borders, so they'd been creeping into Washington state. Their growing numbers and range had caused conflict in the more populous state. Some called for eradicating "pest" wolves while others supported the introduction of the species back into its native environment. If a wolf had killed a person, it could spur the government to lean toward more state-sanctioned killings.

"Did they catch the animal?" I asked. There were still so few of them in the Talol Wilds. I didn't want anyone to hurt one.

"No one knows except for Christy's and my family. They don't want word to get out."

I couldn't understand this crazy decision. "Why?"

"Because Uncle Thomas lived illegally on public land, around Trout Creek outside Colville National Forest. He was a real modern-day hermit in the woods. We were lucky if he visited town every couple of years or so. He didn't like other people, not even his own siblings."

"Then how do you know a wolf killed him?"

"Because Christy's mom insists on texting him regularly to make sure he's okay. He generally responds at least once or twice a week, but after weeks of no contact, she asked me to go check it out."

Oh no. "You found him?"

He nodded.

The hollowness in Vincent's eyes suddenly made sense. I couldn't even imagine what it would be like to find a body mangled by a wolf. "I'm so sorry."

"It's what family does. We take care of each other."

"You at least reported his death, right?"

Vincent laughed without mirth. "I've told you before, my family and Christy's doesn't trust authority. Reporting his death could cause immigration issues with certain members of the family."

"But not saying anything could also get you into a lot of trouble. You're a cop."

He squared his shoulders in defiance. "Sometimes you have to do uncomfortable things in order to protect the people you care about."

Something about his stance told me this went beyond a mere unreported accident. "You've done your part. Let me help you now. Maybe if I take a look at your uncle's campsite, I could find the wolf and determine if he's gone rabid or something."

But Vincent shook his head. "This one stays in the family."

"What's that supposed to mean?"

"It means I'm going to track the wolf down and kill it."

Anger flashed alongside the fire in my pithways. "You can't do that!"

"Why not?"

"Gray wolves are creatures of Nasci. There are precious few of them left as is."

Vincent scowled at me. "This one killed my uncle."

"But you don't know why."

"It killed Uncle Thomas. That's all I need to know."

"He or she"—I emphasized the pronouns to indicate that I saw the wolf as an intelligent being worth of respect—"may have been provoked by a human in his or her territory."

Vincent stiffened. "Do you really hate Christy that much?"

"Of course not!" I purposely clenched my fists so my twitchy fingers wouldn't be tempted to draw a sigil. "But I'm a shepherd of Nasci. I protect all of her creations from harm."

"I didn't come here to listen to your little nature wizard creed."

I resisted the urge to slap him for acting like my life's work was some company slogan. "And I didn't come to condone a straight up illegal poach. Even if you could prove a wolf murdered Christy's uncle, you won't be able to find the exact one who did it. You could slaughter an innocent animal."

"My mind's made up," Vincent glowered. "I'm heading

up north tomorrow, and you can't stop me."

I slid into a sigil stance, hands heavy with earth pith. "Wanna bet?" Bits of sand floated around my boots, attracted to the sudden surge in my pithways.

Vincent's mouth dropped in shock. "Are you threatening me?"

I honestly didn't know, so I didn't answer.

His face reddened. "You know the real reason I came here? To see if there was anything in our relationship to salvage after your breach of trust."

"You think me showing up invited at your family's lunch is a 'breach of trust?'" I asked incredulously. "You've strung trackers in my shoelaces and had my phone bugged with a GPS app."

"And you used magic to douse my mom in iced tea."

I flinched. "I didn't think you saw that."

"Well, I did. I can't wait to hear why you felt that was necessary."

He was right. I'd made a stupid, impulsive decision, no matter how much his mom had been baiting me at the time. I opened my mouth to apologize.

But then he cut me off. "On second thought, I don't want to hear your excuses. You knew I wanted to keep us secret for a while. Just until I could warm my mom up to the idea that I was never going to date Christy. Now she hates you."

My face burned. I was sick of Vincent worrying about his manipulative ex-wife. All my sympathy evaporated. "What a crying shame," I said in a flat monotone. "However will you manage now that your illicit girlfriend is out to the world?"

"You know what, forget it!" he cried. "My life has been thrown into chaos since you showed up. I'm done! We're done!"

"You can't just stalk off to kill endangered wolves!" I yelled at his back. "I'll follow you to Washington!"

He paused to glare at me over his shoulder. "And

abandon all your friends guarding the lesions you allowed Rafe to create? Yeah, you're right. That sounds like something you would do."

I winced. That accusation hurt. My involvement with Rafe had caused a lot of grief, but I'd convinced myself I had to move forward. I couldn't change the past. I just had to live with it.

I'd thought Vincent understood that.

As he stalked back up the hill, I couldn't help myself. All my pent-up anger and frustration came out in the form of a square with the slash. A pile of sand in front of him suddenly blew up in his face. Vincent coughed as he stepped back, wiping particles off his brow.

I couldn't believe what I'd done. I'd attacked one of the few people I cared about because we were fighting. I sank down to my knees, forcing my hands in the sand where they couldn't draw sigils.

"V…Vincent," I called weakly. "I'm sorry."

He gave me a look of utter disgust. "Stay away from me and my family, Ina."

A heaviness that had nothing to do with earth pith filled my chest. It numbed all my senses as Vincent climbed over a sand dune and vanished out of sight.

CHAPTER 4

I SAT ON the beach by myself for a while, staring blankly at an angry red sun setting behind a turbulent sea. The wind kicked up and blew sand so hard it stung my eyes, nature's karma for my earlier sigil. Dark clouds threatened to the south, easily as black as the oncoming night. A possible storm. Ronan and his seals did not return, either scared off by the change in weather or my obvious distress. Crackles of electricity seeped unbidden into my pithways, jumping from the lightning charm around my neck. I took deep calming breaths to force all that raw energy back out, afraid I would lose control and blast something on accident in my current state.

I'd pushed Vincent away. It shouldn't have surprised me. I failed miserably at relationships, coating myself in a layer of sarcasm and impulsive choices. I'd really believed, though, that Vincent would understand me, even if I made him mad now and again.

But I'd underestimated how much his family meant to him. I love my parents and all, but we have a silent agreement to (mostly) keep out of each other's business. I wouldn't hesitate to go home if necessary, but it was best if my mom and dad didn't know what I did for a living. For their part, although they worried and nagged, they seemed content enough to let me pursue my supposedly carefree life choices.

Vincent's family (and by proxy Christy's) wasn't at all like that. The whole clan got together every Sunday. They knew how many girls Oscar brought home. They understood that a spark of ken ran in their families and were proud of the lives they had built with their talents. Vincent was the non-magical black sheep, scorned for his choice to become a cop. I'd thought he'd pick me over them.

I pulled my knees into an embrace. I guess I'd been wrong.

As I tried desperately to quash the ache I felt about Vincent, one thing became crystal clear. He'd been right that I couldn't rush off to Washington. We had a very serious pressing issue here. Even taking a moment to collect myself on the beach was selfish. Sipho needed those circular saws.

Vincent had to go his own way. I had to go mine.

I forced myself to stand. Shaking off some shoulder tension, I kicked off my footwear and stuffed my socks inside. As my bare toes curled in the moist sand, I closed my eyes and let Nasci's energy flow through me. Coarse earth pith pooled in crevices deep inside me, taking over from the forest dirt I'd absorbed earlier. Salt water stung my tongue and traveled into my core. The sea breeze melted into my skin, sending flurries inside my limbs. I ignited them all to reheat my inner heat sigil, a glow like a campfire raging in my veins. It wasn't quite as refreshing as a soak in the hot spring, but it connected me back to the nature I had vowed to protect.

By the time I opened my eyes, the sun had disappeared, leaving only gold and pink streaks of its light behind. Stars appeared behind me, twinkling in the first hours of true night. The dark clouds, I noticed, had evaporated completely, taking with it the strong winds. I tried to see it as a good omen, that perhaps I had also avoided a major storm by breaking up with a guy outside of Nasci's devoted circle of followers.

Yeah, it was a terrible metaphor. Trudging back toward the wisp channel, I tried to forget everything outside of my control and instead focus on those things where I might actually make a difference: the damned lesions and the vaetturs that would attack them.

* * *

I used a fingerflame to trek my way back to the homestead. It took me a good twenty minutes to locate where I'd stashed the paper bag, and then I accidentally set it ablaze with my lit digit. Luckily, I'm always packing water pith, but the bag was toast. I had to grasp the circular saws to my chest like a schoolgirl hauling textbooks. The blades couldn't cut me in their cases, but the sharp plastic edges drew blood on my forearms twice.

Honestly, though, I welcomed the mounting irritation. Cursing under my breath was preferable to bursting into tears. I apparently roused Kam, Sipho's darker nocturnal cougar, because she met me well outside of the homestead's cloaked borders. Undeterred by my poor attitude, she demanded pats in exchange for letting me move forward.

I dropped the circular saws onto the wet ground to comply. "You know Sipho needs those," I said even as I gave her a proper rubdown. She liked a thorough scratching between her ears and under her chin, but tonight she also shifted so I would scrub down her sides.

It's nice to be wanted, even for the little things.

Once done with me, she abruptly bounded back into the darkness. I picked up my haul and crossed the threshold into the homestead. An ordinary person would have seen me walking through a sheer mountain face, but my vision displayed the last fruit-bearing trees in the

32

orchards, drawing me inward with their neat rows.

I passed through several fields, heading for the forge, the barn-like building with smoke curling out of its chimney. I paid no attention to any of the small ponds dug into the various meadows, which is why I nearly jumped out of my skin when a voice called out from below the shadowed waters.

"Yo, chica! Welcome back."

Stringy hair attached to a round head like some black-and-white movie monster splashed upward to my right. My fingerflame highlighted white teeth and a hooked nose. Only one shepherd in the southern homestead lounged in water instead of chilling at the homestead lodge, especially this late at night.

"Yeesh, Baot. You took off five years of my life."

He held a palm out to me, and my damp hoodie fluttered as water pith came off it. He cocked his head to the side. "You've been to the ocean."

It shouldn't have surprised me that Baot could sense the subtle shift in salt content on my clothes. "Yeah. I saw Ronan. He misses you."

"I miss my seal buddy too," he said with a sigh.

"You just come off a lesion shift?"

"Actually, I'm about to relieve Guntram. I always get stuck with the overnight shifts."

I detected a hint of resentment in the shepherd's usually cheerful demeanor. "Is that a problem?"

He shrunk back a little, chagrined. "I don't mean to complain. I just miss sleeping in the ocean."

I blinked as I processed that statement. "You prefer sleeping underwater rather than on land?"

"I'm used to the extra pressure. Plus, I have a few octopi buddies who sometimes coil themselves around me. It's like being wrapped in a living papoose."

I couldn't reconcile that freaky image, so I pushed it from my mind. "Well, sorry it's been a while. Hopefully this will change things." I shifted the square plastic cases in my arms, one nicking me near the elbow for good measure. "I'm on my way to deliver new supplies to Sipho."

Baot pushed some hair out of his face so he could eyeball the circular saws. "You think it'll be enough to seal the three lesions?"

I wished I could reassure him. Even though we'd only been stuck guarding lesions for a few weeks, the unrelenting effort was beginning to take its toll on all of us. "I honestly don't know. But Sipho's working day and night on it."

Baot heard the worry in my voice and nodded reassuringly. "If anyone can do it, it's our forger."

"Catch ya later, Baot."

"Bye, ya." Then he dove back under the water, an impressive feat given the deepest part of the pond was only four feet.

None of the other shepherds deserved all this extra stress, I thought as I approached the forge's dual square doors, the top half ajar. I buried the lingering guilt that Vincent had left in my gut as I used my hip to open the bottom half.

"Hey—" I began to call out.

"Sh!" Sipho hissed. She glanced up at me from the workbench on the opposite side of the room, a playing card-sized sheet of metal in one hand and an etching tool in the other. She'd wound her dark hair into tight braids on her head, a few squiggly strands having broken free at the end of the day. She motioned one bare muscled shoulder toward a slumped figure close to me.

Draped over the sturdy wooden table, I couldn't see Callum's face tucked in his arms, but his dirty hair spiked out in all directions. His loose tunic couldn't hide his gangly limbs, some parts of his adolescent body growing faster than others. Two stacks of haphazard books framed either side of him, stuffed with ribbon bookmarks. He snorted at my entrance, but he soon settled back down to a comfortable rhythm. Nur, the lighter colored mountain lion, though, glared at me from his feet, as if to say, "Thanks, loudmouth."

I gingerly tiptoed over to Sipho and laid the circular saws on her workstation. "Sorry," I whispered.

"He fell asleep doing some research on the next etch I might try."

Callum often harvested the fields while Sipho kept plugging away at the damp wards to seal the lesion. He'd been laboring all morning before I left to help Oscar. Honestly, I have no idea what our homestead would have done without the forger's new apprentice. With the rest of us so busy, we would have lost the fall harvest for sure.

"He definitely deserves a night off," I said, more as a comment to myself than any sort of rebuke.

Sipho took it the wrong way. "I tell him to go to sleep every night, but he insists on helping with the sigils," she said with such vehemence that Nur growled.

I raised my hands in self-defense. "I didn't mean anything by it. Just that he's working hard like we all are."

Sipho slouched a little. "My apologies. I'm very frustrated that I haven't been able to find a ward design to meet our needs yet."

"I take it your last prototype fizzled."

"It was worse than its predecessor, if you can believe it. I could sense Nasci's lifeblood a fathom away with it in place." Sipho rubbed her temples in frustration. "I don't understand why I can't plug the lesion's flow."

I sat next to her on the bench. "At least you're not to blame for opening them in the first place."

Sipho removed her hands from her head. "And neither are you. You are not blaming yourself for Rafe's actions again, are you?"

"Not really, but…" I thought of Vincent's scowling face. My heart sank down into my ankles.

Sipho laid a hand over mine and squeezed. "We cannot erase the past, but we certainly can learn from it." She waved a hand at a dozing Callum. "We never would have found him without you."

I snorted. "Hooray. I'm the harbinger of child labor."

"He is better off honing his Nasci-given talents than being bounced around from place to place." Callum had been one of those kids who slips through the cracks in our foster care system.

"I guess," I said uncertainly.

"No, it is true," Sipho insisted. "He's not only tending the fields but learning how to be a true forger. Elif never would have given me access to such knowledge at such a young age. I was truly only a farmhand for my first years as an apprentice."

The more Sipho talked about Elif, the forger who maintained the northern homestead on Mt. Rainier, the less I liked her. Elif viewed her job as chief architect of all the forge work, and she ruled her domain like any bad corporate micromanager. It was one of the many reasons I vowed to do everything possible to preserve our homestead's independence.

I said none of this out loud, not wanting to provoke an obviously tired Sipho. Instead, I stifled a giggle as Callum's snores reached an impressive crescendo. "Glad the kid's pulling his weight."

"And you are too. If you believe in nothing else, believe in that." Then Sipho let go of my hand to appreciate the circular saws I'd brought. "This will keep me supplied for at least a week."

I stood. "Be careful opening those things. The edges are wicked sharp."

Sipho lifted her left hand to show me a cloth strip she'd tied around the base of her thumb, a homemade bandage. "Tell me about it."

CHAPTER 5

I EXPECTED AZAR the fire shepherd to wake me up at the butt crack of dawn for a lesion shift. I'd been relieved from duty yesterday to buy Sipho's supplies, but I wouldn't have that excuse today. I didn't mind pulling my weight, but I hated seeing the wrong side of dawn. Azar knew this and had no qualms being my alarm clock. I hadn't decided yet if her calm threats delivered in a scary monotone were better or worse than Guntram's bluster.

Imagine my surprise then when I woke instead to an insistent vibration somewhere around my midsection. Blinking in confusion with a drool-slathered cheek, my brain tried to reconcile the mid-morning songbirds with the irritating hum. It was then I realized it was my phone in my hoodie's kangaroo pouch.

Someone was calling me.

Desperate to hear from Vincent, I scrambled for the phone. I found it just in time to miss the call entirely. The phone's screen flickered dark. I frantically clicked the home button only to find a missed call from my mother.

Cursing my bad luck, I tossed the phone on the scratchy mattress and moaned while picking loose straw from the mattress out of my hair. The last thing I wanted to do was talk to my mom, but I couldn't contain my curiosity. My mom rarely called. Trying not to imagine some extra disaster crashing down on my life, I listened to the playback.

"Gene, I'm worried about you. At least when you had a credit card, I knew you were still alive. Now I never know what you're up to. We ordered a new card for you with a lower spending limit. Come home and pick it up whenever you have a chance."

I listened to the message again, savoring the bitter irony of it all. My mom had cut me off from the family lines of credit after she discovered I'd charged too many restaurant dates with Vincent. Now, after working my tail off for Oscar and having broken up with Vincent, she offered me a new one. Perfect timing.

I considered not dropping by at all and letting my mom stew. I had a source of income now, ridiculous though it was, and I didn't need my parents' financial help anymore. But I recognized the desperation in her voice. I should probably go pick up the stupid card and use it once in a while before she went into full-blown panic mode and called the cops to do a welfare check on me.

And yeah, I recognized she did this because she cared and all. That more than anything helped motivate me out of bed and into the lodge hallway.

All the other bedrooms' doors were open. Likewise, no one stirred in the kitchen or common area with its dirt floor, pool of water, and always-lit fireplace. I wondered who else was at the homestead besides me. I grabbed a homemade granola bar from a batch Euchloe must have made because it tasted like bark, then walked outside to a cool but sunny fall day. Besides smoke curling from the forge, there was no sign of anyone else.

But the animals were out and about. Canada geese honked in a V-formation above me, heading south for the winter. A wild jackrabbit bolted out of a cornfield. I was confused what had startled the poor thing when Nur came bounding out after her. The cougar gave the jackrabbit a decent chase, but the cat paused enough times to make it clear to me he wouldn't actually kill the bunny. Sipho frowned upon any hunting directly inside the homestead boundaries, and her cats generally obeyed that rule. Nur's prey, however, didn't know that. The poor thing squealed as she scurried back into the underbrush.

Ridiculous as Nur's antics were, the thing that really caught my eye was a flash of orange in a wooded area away from the farm fields. I counted a dozen rough-skinned newts scurrying farther into the trees. Animals wandered into the homestead at their leisure, but that many newts had to be Azar's kidama.

I pursued their bumpy skins at a distance, only catching glimpses of them when they twisted to expose bright underbellies. Azar had only recently become an augur, but she took her new position very seriously. Her elevated position was vital in proving the southern homestead could still operate on its own. Whenever she wasn't guarding a lesion, she honed her elemental skills. I'd seen her practicing complex techniques into the wee morning hours, the slashing flames from her fingertips more impressive than many industrial fireworks. She poured over books in the library. Baot even told me she'd managed to form a mist over the lodge using insular script, which made my pithways ache just thinking about it.

I kept my distance from the newts, creating a gentle air bubble underneath my boots to stop from crunching any leaves. I wasn't stalking the newts, per se, but I was curious why Azar would hang out so far from the homestead and not wake me up for a lesion shift. When I walked a good half mile past the boundary and into denser forest, my curiosity intensified. I stopped to let the newts cross a shallow creek. Once they scrambled over the opposite embankment, I followed.

As the sound of babbling water receded, I heard a voice. Quiet but confident, I recognized it as Azar's.

"Did the Oracle give us more time?"

A second gruff voice responded, "No."

My pulse quickened. Guntram was out here too? A sudden beating of wings and caws up ahead confirmed it. I crouched low behind a thick cedar, not daring to get any closer for fear of attracting either augur's kidama. I settled in to eavesdrop on this unexpected conversation.

"We are in a precarious position," Guntram said. "It's been weeks, and we have not been able to seal the lesions. The Oracle is not pleased. She says she cannot keep things from Sertalis any longer."

"But Sipho is so close to creating a damp ward."

"Be that as it may, our time has run out. Darby's petition to move Tabitha's Columbia basin territory back to the northern homestead comes up tomorrow at noon. Darby will tell everyone about the lesions then."

I bit my lip to keep myself from making a sound. I'd known that Darby had threatened to defect back to the north, but no one had said it was almost a done deal already.

Azar's normally level voice held sadness. "Then we are doomed."

"You're an augur now," Guntram argued. "And we've acquired a forger apprentice. Our numbers hold up."

Azar's tone remained matter-of-fact as she replied, "But Sertalis views me as a weak addition at best. He's too arrogant to ever believe his own former eyas, and a fire-based one at that, could ever become as powerful as him."

I tried to imagine poor Azar having to train under such an overbearing jerk. He was the kind of guy that exuded an "I'm the smartest person in the room" attitude with arrogance to spare. He made Tabitha's tiger mom training with Darby look almost quaint by comparison.

"What else can we do?" Guntram said. "Maybe if this had happened with Tabitha alive, we could have offered to bind Ina even as a full-blown shepherd to appease him."

The northern homestead labeled me as a problem with

my unusual lightning powers, but to hear Guntram casually suggest excommunicating me stabbed me right in the heart. Coupled with Vincent's rejection, it was too much. I crept back up to a standing position, ready to defend myself even though I just wanted to fry him on the spot.

Fortunately for all involved, Guntram calmed me down with his next words, "Although, I never would have agreed to that. Ina has proven herself one of us. She passed her Shepherd Trial. It is sacrilege to reverse it based on Sertalis's uneasiness over her abilities. The Oracle would have to bind me too."

Whoa. Bind an augur? I sat back down, hugging myself to keep from shivering too hard.

"Agreed," Azar said. "Ina is one of us. She's proven herself beyond all doubt."

I gulped down the lump in my throat as quietly as I could.

"Our last hope is to appeal to the Oracle's empathy," Guntram said. "She knows the Talol Wilds will be weaker as a whole under Sertalis's command."

"I wish I could rely on that, but Sertalis makes too many strong points for consolidation. Tabitha died under our watch. Her former eyas has petitioned to defect to the north. We have a radical shepherd with lightning powers. And to top it all off, we can't seal three lesions attracting stronger and stronger vaetturs from even beyond our borders. Once word of all this comes out to the others, all hope is lost."

"Then what would you have us do?"

Azar's voice took on a hard edge. "I can challenge Sertalis to a duel."

I stiffened. Guntram had told me about shepherd duels. In the more violent old-timey days, shepherds had used them to settle disputes. Someone generally ended up either dead or badly injured. Guntram always made them seem like relics of the past, reiterating we had a hard enough time recruiting new eyases as it was. I didn't know duels were still a thing.

"You cannot do that! It's too risky."

"If I defeat Sertalis, it will prove that the south can defend ourselves."

"At what cost? Azar, trust me when I say I have utmost faith in you, but Sertalis has years of experience. I've worked with him to banish vaetturs that would curl your hair. You are not ready to face someone of his caliber. There's a reason he believes himself the rightful successor should anything happen to the Oracle."

Ugh, no. I'd bind myself if that blowhard was the Talol Wilds Oracle.

Azar harbored a similar sentiment. "He only dreams he could breathe the conjured air around her. You are much more suited to such an important leadership position."

Guntram snorted in derision. "Then perhaps you wish I would challenge Sertalis to a duel?"

"No, you shouldn't. We need you in the south. I'm much more expendable."

"No one is expendable," Guntram snapped. "None of this is worth your life, Azar. You cannot issue a duel."

Azar's voice lowered to an almost childlike whisper as she asked, "Then what will become of us tomorrow?"

"I don't know, but we must have faith that Nasci will guide us."

I tensed as I heard crunching leaves, but they sounded like they were moving away from me. I stay huddled against the tree until I could no longer hear anything, not even Guntram's ravens calling for each other.

I felt as small as Azar's voice. The southern homestead stood on the edge of a nasty cliff. I couldn't see any reason why the northern homestead wouldn't successfully drive us straight over.

And a large chunk of that was my fault.

CHAPTER 6

"WHAT DO YOU think, Ina?"

A part of my subconscious registered Callum's question, but my brain cells had other problems. The two of us had been picking green beans in the garden for the last hour, having mostly filled up a large wicker basket between us. Callum had kept up a steady chatter, but I'd only half-listened, too busy imagining what would happen at the northern homestead tomorrow. Would Guntram really be able to convince the Oracle that we should keep our autonomy? And if not, would Azar risk her own life to stop Sertalis?

I couldn't just sit here and wait to hear what happened at that meeting.

Callum snorted derisively. "You're not even listening."

The teenager's stereotypical moodiness brought me back to the here and now. "Sorry. I'm tired. Can you repeat what you said?"

He pouted but complied with my request. "I really think Sipho and I are missing something crucial in our lesion ward design."

"Maybe it's the sigil you guys are etching or even the stroke order. Magic is finicky like that."

"That's what Sipho says, but a second component might boost the tungsten's dampening effects. She's willing to try anything. Problem is, I've gone through every material we have at the forge. Twice. Nothing works."

"Sounds like you should go shopping."

I knew I'd opened Pandora's box when Callum's eyes sparkled with enthusiasm. "You'll go with me?"

I stifled a groan. The last thing I needed was another embarrassing store trip with a forger in tow. Fortunately, I had an excuse. Sort of. "I don't have time today. I'm on lesion guard duty tonight."

Callum huffed. "Making the wards can't wait."

"You could go shopping on your own, you know."

"I can?"

I flashed him a teasing grin. "Haven't you ever gone to a store by yourself?"

"Of course!" he flung back, insulted. "It's just that you insisted on going with Sipho, so I thought I'd need someone with me too."

"Sipho's been living outside civilization for too long. She's not as consumer savvy as you are. Plus, she was looking for a specific item. Sounds like you'd be browsing. You can do that on your own."

He brightened a little. "I guess that's true." Then his smile faltered. "But I don't have money."

I rooted around in my hoodie pouch and flashed him a few twenty-dollar bills. "You know how to wisp channel back into town from here?"

Callum nodded. "I can get to Eugene. I'll go after we finish this and see what I can find."

I handed him the bills. "Don't lose those, okay? Cash is hard to come by." Then I lowered my voice dramatically. "But if you happen to buy yourself some cheap food on your trip, I promise not to tell anyone."

Callum held up his fist for a conspiratorial bump. I didn't leave him hanging.

With a plan in motion, Callum whirled through the rest

of the harvest. We lugged the heavy basket to the storage shed together. We placed it into an etched wooden box that acted as a refrigerator. Then Callum wished me luck with guard duty and skipped off to tell Sipho where he was going.

Technically, I had lied to Callum. I didn't have guard duty tonight. At least not yet. But I went off to find Baot, hoping to rectify that situation.

Even though there were many ponds scattered throughout the property, Baot favored the larger, deeper ones. I located him at my second guess. I had to dive down to the bottom to find him. He was sleeping, and although I hated to wake him, I thought he'd like to hear what I had to say. I nudged him until he snorted bubbles and opened his eyes.

"Ina?" he yawned.

Since I couldn't talk underwater like he could, I urged him to the surface so we could chat. I plopped my butt onto a rock and wrote a drying sigil as Baot stood chest deep in the pond.

Most other shepherds (myself included) would have been grumpy from such an interruption, but Baot was annoyingly perky as he asked, "What can I do for you, chica?"

"Could I switch guard duty with you?"

"Is something wrong?"

I queued up the explanation I'd devised while harvesting the green beans. "It bothers me you can't sleep overnight in the ocean because you always pull the overnight shift. Well, I'm supposed to watch the Mohawk lesion from mid-morning until dusk tomorrow. Maybe we could switch shifts?"

"Wow, that's really nice of you, but Guntram already rearranged the schedules quite a bit for tomorrow."

"He did?" This was news to me.

Baot nodded. "He assigned double shifts to both Zibel and Euchloe at the other lesions. They're stuck there until sunset tomorrow."

"Did he say why?"

"Only that he and Azar will be unavailable tomorrow afternoon. He didn't give any more concrete details than that."

Of course, he didn't. Guntram didn't want the rest of us to worry about trouble brewing in the north.

Well, I didn't plan on sitting on the sidelines for this one. Not when so much was at stake, and I'd caused some of it.

"Guntram didn't tell me any of that. I was going to relieve you tomorrow morning. So, shifting our schedules shouldn't make a big difference."

"You're right. It shouldn't." Baot beamed. "Thanks. I really appreciate it."

"Don't thank me. Just enjoy a night snuggling with your octopus buddies."

* * *

Against all logic, the deep woods at night are creepy to shepherds, even though we have nothing to fear from them. Normal animals recognize us as peers of Nasci, fighting against the creatures of Letum for their protection. Still, I don't think you can be human and not feel a sense of doom wandering by yourself in near pitch-black darkness under bony branches and whistling winds. It's written somewhere deep in our DNA, and while you can ignore it, it never goes away completely.

But you can mostly ignore it under a dazzling display of galaxy-encrusted stars. I shivered, but my heat sigil kept me physically warm. I huddled near the bottom of a gully with a creek running through it, several feet away from the patch of bare dirt where vegetation refused to grow. The lesion even looked like a scar under my fingerflame.

While usually I would keep my distance from the lesions, not having the pith sensitivity like the forgers to sense the leak itself, I couldn't keep myself from examining it tonight. Using an earth sigil, I even plunged both hands into the dirt, willing myself to sense what Sipho and Callum did when they came to examine it. The dirt did feel funny in my hand, maybe a little unnatural, as if it had been made in a factory. But that could have been my overactive imagination from sitting a few hours by myself with nothing but the scurrying of nocturnal animals to keep me company.

A sudden bout of loneliness overcame me. I wished I could call Vincent.

I withdrew my hands from the lesion. I tried my hardest to keep him as far from my thoughts as possible, but he'd become so intertwined with my life, it was hard not to rely on him. I'd almost left my cell phone back at the lodge, just to resist feeling the heavy weight of possible contact with him, but in the end, I couldn't bear to part with it.

Not yet. Not with everything fresh.

A loud snapping of twigs shot adrenaline through my system. I clasped my air charm instinctively, crouching low to the ground with feet shoulder width apart, ready to draw a sigil.

But the noise turned out to be a black-tailed deer wandering along the creek bed. Her eyes flashed glassy in the dark. I enlarged my fingerflame to make out a sleek coat with a tuft of white running down her chest.

I should have known.

"Why do you guys hang around the lesions?" I called to her.

I don't know what I expected. It's not like the deer could answer back.

I dismissed the deer with a frustrated wave. "Tabitha's not here anymore. You should go."

The deer wheezed at me, a sharp vocalization that made me wince. Then in an exaggerated leap, she bounded back into the forest.

Once I got my heart rate down, I muttered, "Sure. Be that way." But my lackluster attempt at humor didn't lift my unease as I continued to stand guard for the rest of the night. I'm not sure what bothered me most: the unnaturally dead patch of earth, Tabitha's kidama keeping watch over it, or tomorrow's meeting on Mt. Rainier.

CHAPTER 7

AS I STEPPED onto the northern homestead's main path, mountain spring gurgling at my side, I realized I had no idea what I was doing.

After Baot relieved me from lesion duty, I'd booked it to Mt. Rainier. It was nearly noon. The petition meeting would begin at any moment. I'd entered from the lower slopes, following the creek that eventually paralleled the beaten road. I could either go right and travel toward the fancy buildings that made up the homestead proper, or I could go left and pass fields and orchards until I reached the Oracle's remote longhouse. Earlier this summer, I'd argued a petition at the Oracle's residence, so I jogged in that direction.

Although Sipho maintained a decent-sized farm, the northern homestead had easily twice as much ground to cover with a lot more exotic plants than the standard vegetables and fruits you'd find at a local farmer's market. In between the carrots and potatoes, I saw rows of leafy daikon radishes poking out of the ground. The orchards had apples, but also orange trees and even a few viny dragon fruit cacti. Intricate sigils had been carved carefully into each plant, helping it regulate moisture and absorb different nutrients from the soil. You could say a lot about Elif (and I did), but she ran a tight ship.

I'd almost made it past one of the last orchards when a voice called out to me. "Where are you going, lightning shepherd?"

I froze in my tracks as a stocky, robed figure walked toward me from between rows of filbert trees, their thick branches sprouting almost directly from the ground like a living waterspout. She carried a pole over her shoulders, from which hung two overflowing baskets full of nuts on either end. The pole bowed, showing how heavy the weight was.

I didn't get a good look at the person's face until she placed her load on the ground and wiped the sweat from her brow. Dirt coated her skin, making it hard to determine the original complexion. Light wrinkles indicated she had to be leaning toward Guntram's age.

It wasn't until she flashed her cobalt blue eyes at me that I recognized her as one of the northern homestead's forger apprentices.

"I don't know if we've formally met," I said. "But you obviously recognize me."

She grinned, her teeth surprisingly white. "Everyone knows you. You're all anyone's been gossiping about up here for weeks."

Great. I'd become a local celebrity, and not the good kind. "I've come to listen to the petition."

"Then you're going the wrong way." She pointed back toward the mountain. "Everyone's gathered in the amphitheater. You should run along, or you'll miss the entire thing."

"What about you? Shouldn't you be there?"

"I'd like to." She'd already lifted the pole back on her shoulders. "But the trees don't harvest themselves. There's always work for ol' Oduvan to do."

Only old or crazy people talk about themselves in third person. But she seemed nice enough, and she'd treated me with respect. It was a lot more than I expected at the northern homestead.

"I'm sure you can take a break and come," I told her. "I'll even come back and help you harvest afterward, if you want me to."

Oduvan nearly dropped her pole. "You'd work the harvest?"

"Of course. I help Sipho in the southern homestead all the time. It's no big deal."

"It's not how things are done here," Oduvan said. "I am grateful to serve Nasci in this small way."

Despite the conviction in her voice, it sounded bogus to me. "Are you sure? Because it's really no problem for me."

"No, lightning shepherd, I will finish my chores alone. But I do thank you." She turned to head farther back into the orchard.

"Thank you for telling me about the meeting," I called to her. And then as an afterthought, I added, "The name's Ina."

She paused to bow her head. "Oduvan," she supplied, I guess in case I hadn't caught it before. Then she sauntered off.

I made my way toward the amphitheater. I passed the first metal mast that served as a lamp, the road completely empty. No one milled around the grand northern buildings—the gymnasium, hostel, or library—all recessed away from the road among the thick trees. I'd only visited the northern homestead a handful of times, but there was always at least one or two people roaming about. I guess today was special.

The amphitheater had only a single entrance which led into its topmost row. Like a druidic twist on the Greek stages of old, the amphitheater leveraged the mountain's naturally steep slopes to create concentric semicircles down to a focal platform at the bottom. Uneven rock benches allowed seating for an intimate fifty or so people.

Beyond the platform, a photographer's dream snapshot stretched to the horizon, a mixture of barren and grassy hills that ebbed and flowed like waves, fluffy clouds accentuating the view overhead.

The Oracle (real name "Yoi," even though Guntram hated when I called her that) stood in the foreground of this magnificent backdrop, ten or so people sitting close to her in the front row, their backs to me. I recognized Guntram and Azar right away with their signature tattered cloak and olive-green attire respectively. Most of the northern shepherds wore the generic dreary gray tones of the northern homestead, which I always felt make them look like cultists of Cthulhu.

The only exceptions: Sertalis and Elif.

Sertalis was the perfect combination of an accomplished illusionist and that teacher who hated your guts the minute you walked into his classroom. He had his face in partial profile, revealing a trim mustache to match his deep brown hair with white tips at the temples. His short black tunic had gold-colored trim at the cuffs. Beside him with a ramrod straight posture to rival any medieval princess sat Elif. She too wore black robes, but it served to only contrast with her shock white hair cut in a severe bob and slightly grayish skin. Her dark eyes focused on the Oracle like a hawk, not so much surveying as gauging prey.

The Oracle appeared positively serene next to their disapproving scowls. With a heavily wrinkled face on top of a navy tunic with bright blue and purple beads, she blended wisdom and strength while still exuding cheerfulness. She wore a skirt that reached down to her ankles, ruffling in the breeze. Despite looking old enough to own a walker or two, she moved with fluid grace across the platform as she spoke. She noticed me enter, but as I slid into a seat in the back row, she made no mention of my arrival.

"…understand my decision," she was saying. "Tabitha guarded the Columbia River Basin since her augur passed on, as did her augur before her. It has been something of a tradition for the previous augur to hand down the territory through a handpicked mentoring line, and I am loath to end that today."

Guntram stood from his bench, his back to me. "Our objection does not stem from Darby taking over the land. She is a very competent shepherd, one of the best skilled in earth pith in a generation, and we are sorry to lose her. We respect her wish, so long as the northern homestead also respects the south's desire to remain a separate governing entity."

Sertalis swiftly rose to his feet. "If Darby transfers the land to us, the south's territory will shrink significantly. It is a waste to maintain two homesteads at that point."

Guntram shifted slightly to face him. "It is not a waste. We've been successful for over a decade."

"You'd call Tabitha's death a success?" he sneered.

The Oracle raised a hand. "Shepherds are lost to Letum, Sertalis. We have gone over this. You shall not use that as an argument for combining the homesteads."

Sertalis's lips tightened, obviously not agreeing with the Oracle's sentiment, but he moved on. "What about their lack of a second-in-command?"

Guntram laid a hand on Azar's shoulder before she could stand. "We have a second augur now, as you well know."

"I was talking about a real leader," Sertalis threw back. "One with experience. But I suppose you are fond of freshly minted upstarts in the south."

I couldn't see Azar's face, but the red bracelet she wore glowed orange in her lap, a sure sign she was holding back fire. A sudden breeze also broke through the amphitheater, rustling everyone's hair. Given the balled fists at Guntram's side, I felt pretty confident who had conjured them.

The Oracle took note. "Both of you, please sit down." When the two men reluctantly returned to the stone benches, she addressed the entire congregation. "I will honor the original agreement. The southern homestead is permitted to operate independently with two augurs as long as they can effectively banish all threats from Letum."

That's when Sertalis elbowed the slouching figure to his left. The shepherd reluctantly stood, limp strands of platinum hair falling outside her hood.

My heart raced. Darby. She'd been wearing Tabitha's fur-lined cloak for so long, I hadn't recognized her in the generic northern gray robe. Her normally well-maintained ringlets had apparently loosened with her standards. She looked tired and worn, no longer the beautiful younger half of the Sassy Squad. Sertalis nudged her again, and she lifted her drooping chin.

"Oracle." She cleared her throat, starting soft but growing firm as she gained steam. "As stated in my petition, the very reason I decided to transfer is that I no longer believe the south can adequately guard against the forces of Letum."

A few generic robes whispered in alarm to one another. Sertalis leaned forward eagerly with elbows on his knees. Elif could not quite hide her subtle smirk, so she must have known what was coming too.

The Oracle frowned but waved at Darby. "Can you elaborate on this opinion?"

"When the bound shepherd Rafe emerged from Mt. Hood, he gained the ability to tear into Nasci, rending the earth and absorbing her lifeblood to become more powerful. Although the south managed to bind Rafe, those spots remain as open wounds today. These so-called lesions are attracting vaetturs in droves. I have witnessed the effects of this energy on two separate vaetturs, both of which became more aggressive and gained new abilities to prey upon our world. The south even had to recruit the help of a Bitai Wilds shepherd to stop a recent chumal swarm that sensed Nasci's lifeblood from hundreds of miles away."

Gasps erupted among those who hadn't heard this story. I gritted my teeth. Darby hadn't even helped us with the chumal swarm, the little snitch.

Darby continued. "The south cannot contain this dire threat. Three lesions have opened so far, but many other spots that Rafe defiled remain. I myself have kept a close eye on a potential lesion in the Columbia Gorge because I worry it could rip open at any moment. The southern forger is trying to create a damp ward to seal them, but so far has been unsuccessful. Neither she nor Guntram will ask the north for aid. The south's independent streak could very well cause a swarm of vaettur outbreaks across the Talol Wilds, the likes of which we have never seen before."

One of the gray robes stood. "Did you know of this, Oracle?"

The Oracle nodded. "Yes."

Another stood. "This is outrageous. You cannot let the south operate independently if they can't seal the lesions immediately."

The Oracle held up placating hands. "You must remember that Rafe had been plaguing the north for years before his more insidious attack on the south. The southern homestead did not use that as proof to consolidate all leadership under their authority."

That statement kicked up a hornet's nests of protest among the rest of the northern homestead. They all stood and began defending their efforts at once.

"We did what we could with half the resources!"

"We at least kept Rafe from harming Nasci."

"Rafe was Guntram's problem to begin with."

The Oracle did not need to shout. She tensed, and without so much as twitching a finger, the ground shook. A wind gust stormed through the benches. The ambient air temperature rose several degrees.

Everyone got the hint and sat down, including Darby, effectively cowed.

As the Oracle relaxed, the world restored itself to a calm autumn day. "I do agree that this is a serious situation. One that does warrant extreme measures."

Azar stirred. Guntram turned to her in alarm, shaking his head, but she kept her entire focus on the Oracle.

I gripped my lightning charm, its pith sizzling up my arm. The Oracle wouldn't do it. She couldn't force us to work under the north. So many people I cared about would be screwed into a lifetime of servitude.

But the Oracle merely sighed. "I hoped for some sort of reconciliation, but I wonder if that's impossible now. Perhaps I should seriously consider the consolidation of the entire Talol Wilds."

Azar leaped to her feet, opening her mouth to speak. "Oracle, I—"

She was going to challenge Sertalis. I imagined Azar burning under Sertalis's fire, his wrath and experience bringing her to her knees. Everything inside me clenched and then released out into the wild. A lightning bolt crashed across the sky directly above us, the ensuing thunder drowning out the rest of Azar's words.

Blinded by the sudden charge, everyone in the amphitheater stumbled to their feet, blinking. Most of them had never seen the business end of my lightning magic before. Once they regained their senses, it would be utter chaos.

Which is why I only had seconds to act.

"I challenge Sertalis to a shepherd duel!" I screamed.

CHAPTER 8

I GOT EXACTLY what I deserved, given that I'd tossed a deadly energy surge on top of a nature wizard pow-wow. The uneven stones beneath the benches parted, rocks creeping over my ankles to lock me in place. A ring of fire flashed around me, obscuring my view of the others. The flames licked close enough that I drew a sigil to keep from getting burned. Beyond the wall, angry voices shouted on top of each other, scrambling for control.

But it was a calm voice amplified by a deafening air sigil that rose above the rest. "Quiet," the Oracle whispered harshly, a ghostly echo that caused the hairs on the back of my neck to rise.

As the flames dissipated, I faced off against an angry line of gray robes in sigil stances. Their scowls contrasted with the Oracle's more neutral expression as she wrote the last sigil to push the stones back, releasing me. On her right side, Guntram looked like he wanted to strangle me. On her left, Sertalis had a similar expression but backed by flames in his irises that promised more genuine follow through.

The Oracle's stare seemed to bore into my soul. "Ina has issued a shepherd duel to Sertalis. What objection do you raise to his motives?"

Uh-oh. This sounded more like formal court proceedings than the "let's go fight out back" scenario I'd assumed. I took a stab in the dark. "His hatred of the southern homestead."

The Oracle raised an eyebrow. "You wish to change Sertalis's feelings with a duel?"

Well, no. I expected Sertalis to hate us forever for not being under his grimy little thumb. "I just want him to leave us alone."

I was botching this up badly. Azar lifted her head from a face palm. "Oracle, if I may, I had meant to raise my own challenge before Ina's interruption."

"We will handle one thing at a time," the Oracle said.

Azar flashed me a withering glare meant to melt me in my boots. It did pack a punch, but again, I'm pretty sure Sertalis was further ahead of her in line.

The Oracle tried again. "Ina, please state plainly what you wish to accomplish from this duel."

I straightened my shoulders. "To allow the southern homestead to operate independently from the north."

Sertalis snarled. "This is a farce. The little lightning shepherd thinks she can waltz in here and interrupt our proceedings."

The Oracle lifted her nose. "Are you afraid of a shepherd of lower rank?"

He took a half-step back. "Of course not."

"Do you accept the challenge then?"

The Oracle had put Sertalis in a tough position. Sertalis clearly didn't want to participate in my surprise duel, but if he didn't, it would make him look like a coward. Since he had mountains of experience over me, the only thing he could be scared of was my lightning pith, which he claimed invalidated me as a follower of Nasci.

Ha! Go get 'em, Yoi.

"Yes," Sertalis accepted through tight lips.

"Then state your terms."

Sertalis glowered at me. "If I win, the southern homestead accepts the authority of the north."

"That is not something Ina can acquiesce. Unlike you, she does not have augur standing."

"There is nothing else I desire from this charade," he objected. "It is an equivalent request to hers and should be treated as such."

Unfortunately for my sinking stomach, the Oracle nodded. "I agree. It would have made a lot more sense for an augur of the southern homestead to issue the duel."

Azar raised her head hopefully.

"However," the Oracle continued, "I will allow the highest-ranking augur of the southern homestead to consider if he wishes to honor Ina as their champion in this regard."

Everyone shifted toward Guntram, who folded his arms over his chest. I threw my hands up in despair but managed only a string of muttered curses instead of an outburst. If Guntram got to choose, there wasn't a scruple's chance in a politician's speech he would let me go through with this.

Even so, I didn't expect his reply. "I'll take Ina's place."

Azar gasped. It took me a few more seconds to register what he'd said.

"No!" I yelled. "He can't do that!"

That harsh augmented whisper slammed into my eardrums. "He can. Do not interrupt."

I fell backward on a stone bench, stunned and shaking.

"Guntram, do you accept the terms of this duel with Sertalis?"

"I do," he said above the murmuring of the rest of the crowd.

"Then will you both come forward?"

The pair kneeled down at the Oracle's feet like knights at a queen's beckoning. The Oracle wrote a sigil in the air that created a strange glowing blue smoke wherever her fingers traced.

"It is so declared that augur Sertalis and augur Guntram will decide the fate of the southern homestead. Sertalis's victory will merge the two homesteads while Guntram's victory will keep them separate."

Dust sprinkled down from that strange mist upon the heads of both augurs, sparking like flint on steel as it covered them. Neither of the men flinched, though.

"Henceforth, the pact cannot be broken. A loss is triggered by forfeiture, grave injury, or death by either party. Do you swear upon your sacred vows to uphold this pledge?"

Azar looked like someone had slapped her. I didn't even bother wiping the tears streaking down my cheeks.

"Then I seal the pact above you with the essence of our beloved goddess. You shall both duel at a time and place of my choosing. May Nasci have mercy on your souls."

* * *

The Oracle discussed a few other things, but my poor numb ears only caught a snippet. Something about a vaettur running amok in Okanogan National Forest. I barely cared, haunted that I might have just set my former mentor on a date with death.

With nothing left to talk about, the Oracle declared Darby's petition in limbo until after the duel and dismissed everyone. Azar and Guntram stayed behind, having a heated discussion with wild gestures but low voices. I remained seated as the generic gray robes scooted past me out of the amphitheater first. They cast me a few furtive glances from beneath their hoods but didn't dare address me with the Oracle trailing on their heels. The elderly shepherd gave me a vague smile. I had no idea what she thought of my stunt, and frankly, I had other things to worry about.

Darby left with Sertalis next. She held her head high, ignoring me, the traitor. Sertalis grimaced as if I were a dead bird some neighbor's cat had left on his front lawn. You know, the usual.

Elif was the only one who confronted me directly. She sniffed disdainfully from the aisle, several yards away. "What puddle have you been rolling around in?"

I didn't miss a beat. "One of the pristine pools on your homestead."

She ignored the jab, leaning forward to assess me from head to foot. "You reek of Nasci's befouled presence. Did you come straight here from one of these lesions?"

I hated to admit how impressive it was that Elif could sense the lesion on my clothes from so far away. Trying to access my inner Guntram, I kept my mouth shut.

She narrowed her eyes at me. "You've really made a muck of things, haven't you? No wonder Darby wishes to return to the true fold. Anyone with half a brain would run screaming from your foolishness."

I couldn't let that one slide. "What, so we can all follow your orders like indentured servants? Why have brains at all if you don't let anyone use them?"

Instead of showing anger, she sneered at me. "I'll let you answer that, little shepherd, after Guntram loses the duel." Then she drifted off.

Arrogant bureaucrats one, Ina zero. Or maybe they had more points already. Who was keeping score anyway?

The southern augurs must have finished their discussion because Azar was nowhere in sight. Only Guntram remained, walking between the benches toward me.

He gestured next to me. "Mind if I sit?"

I shrugged. "I'd say it's a free country, but I'm not sure that's actually true around here."

Guntram groaned like the senior citizen he was as he plopped down next to me.

"Your geriatric sighs aren't helping me imagine you kicking Sertalis's butt."

"Are you upset with me too?"

"Of course, I am! If you recall, I volunteered myself as tribute. I didn't expect you to go all 'Girl on Fire' on me."

"Huh? Are you referring to Azar?"

"Never mind." So much for joking around with someone who hadn't had a brush with pop culture since the Elvis years. "It was my mess. I should fix it. Besides, the southern homestead needs you as an augur. I'm more expendable."

He lifted a bushy eyebrow. "Those words sound awfully familiar. Almost as if someone eavesdropped on a recent conversation between me and the 'Girl on Fire.'"

Whoops. I hadn't meant to be so obvious. "I...I..."

"Don't bother trying to explain it away. One of my ravens spotted you yesterday. I worried you might have heard a little too much, but I never imagined you'd show up unannounced to take on Sertalis by yourself."

"I wasn't planning to! But when Azar stood to challenge him, I couldn't stop myself."

Guntram sighed. "Then you can relieve yourself of one burden, Ina. I made up my mind long before your rash appeal that if Azar challenged Sertalis, I would take her place. Today's outcome would have happened one way or another, with or without you."

"Does Azar know?"

"Yes. She reacted about as positively as you are now."

I squeezed my hands together in my lap. "When will the Oracle schedule the duel?"

"If you were paying any attention, you'd know not for a while yet. A good chunk of the north is out hunting an elusive vaettur. Protecting Nasci's creatures must come before our petty differences."

I couldn't keep the quiver out of my voice. "I don't want you to get hurt."

He frowned. "Are you seriously worried for my well-being? I've been at this since before you were born."

"You're tough, Jichan. I'd put my money on you against almost any vaettur, but Sertalis isn't a mindless monster searching for grub. He'll hurt you to get his way."

"I suppose he can try." Guntram surprised me by giving me a wink. "Although I have it on good authority that ravens sometimes eat snakes, not the other way around."

"Really?" I asked, exasperated. "You're finally cracking jokes now?"

"Seems to work out fine for you." He stood, offering me a hand up. "Duel or not, we still have lesions to guard. When's your next shift?"

"Not until tomorrow. I just finished an overnight."

He glanced back at the horizon. "Will you come back to Sipho's with me?"

I thought of my mom's voicemail message. This might be the best chance I'd get for a while to pick up the credit card. "Actually, since I'm in the vicinity, I'd like to catch up with my folks in Lynnwood first."

Guntram nodded. "Don't stay too long. We'll need you back soon. Things are probably going to get worse before they get better."

CHAPTER 9

I WISH GUNTRAM wouldn't jinx us like that, but he was right. Sooner or later, the hammer would fall. I just hoped it didn't take my mentor out with it.

But one disaster at a time. I knocked on the door of my parents' blue split-level house, the sharp scent of fresh mulch assaulting my nostrils. The landscapers must have recently come by to spruce up the front yard. My parents worked odd hours—my mother as a retail store manager and my father as an economics professor at a community college—so I never knew when they'd be home.

My father opened the door. Dad looked like a salaryman plucked straight out of Tokyo: dressed in a suit and tie, wire-framed glasses, and socks because only heathens wore shoes in the house.

He blinked to make sure I didn't disappear like a mirage. "Imogene?"

"Hiya," I said, responding to my birth name. "Mom called and told me to pick up a new credit card. She around?"

He shook his head. "She's closing tonight. You just missed her."

Score! Dealing with Dad would be like getting prison

time reduced to probation. I scooted inside and kicked off my hiking boots. "Darn it. I missed her."

"I'll tell her you dropped by." He wandered into the kitchen and rifled through a stack of envelopes. He found one and handed it to me. "Here you go."

I took it, feeling the hard, rectangular plastic inside. "Thanks." Then my stomach rumbled, reminding me I'd eaten very little today. "Say, you want to go grab a late lunch or something?"

He gestured toward his briefcase by the garage door. "I wish I could, but I've got class soon. I was about to pour myself some coffee and go. Would you like a cup?"

"Sure." I wasn't going to reject a consolation prize. Plus, I could raid the fridge and fix something before I left anyway.

He scurried around the dark kitchen cabinets. I sat on a stool next to the counter, my sole resting on a foot rung so I could bounce my knee up and down.

Dad stirred sugar and milk into a mug, remembering my preferences. "What's going on in your life?"

How does a child begin to tell their clueless parent that they're dealing with mythical monsters and magical politics? Answer: they don't. "The usual. How about you?"

Unlike my mother, my dad didn't pry. "The semester's just started, so I'm still learning names."

"I don't know why you bother." My dad taught over two hundred students a term in his large intro economics courses.

"Because it creates a connection between me and them. Every little bit helps."

But most don't appreciate it. College kids get so angry when you can't remember their names, even when they forget your face the minute they walk out the door. "Well, kudos to you for trying."

"Besides that, I have some sad family news. Your Aunt Fumiko died."

"Oh, that's too bad." I tried to put some emotion

behind my words, but it was hard when you didn't really know the person. Kind of like his students, Dad tried to keep a connection with our Japan-based relatives, even though he himself had been born in America. I'd traveled with him once as a tween to meet them, but I was much more interested in Japan's crazy game arcades than drinking green tea with the older generation at the time.

"Which one was she again?"

"You never met her. She was your grandma's sister, never married. She hadn't been mentally well in a long time."

"Alzheimer's?" I asked, taking a swig of coffee.

Dad hesitated, as if he shouldn't say it. "They believed she was possessed by a kitsune."

The liquid went down the wrong pipe and I choked. Dad patted me on the back until I could speak again.

I'd researched kitsune recently but hadn't learned a whole bunch. Now this just dropped in my lap. "You think Aunt Fumiko was possessed by a Japanese fox spirit?"

My father shifted into lecture mode. "You'd be surprised how hard old beliefs die. Your grandmother absolutely believed in kitsune. She claimed a ninko, an invisible fox spirit, possessed some of our female ancestors, entering them through their fingernails through bolts of lightning."

A chill went through me at that very relevant image. "That's crazy," I mumbled.

"Aunt Fumiko claimed to have all sorts of strange powers: see ghosts, talk to animals, predict storms. It eventually drove her insane, and the family had to commit her to a group home."

A tremor swept over me. "Why didn't you ever mention any of this before?"

"You always had a big imagination, and this is a sad family story. I didn't want you to mistake her condition as anything other than mental illness. Still, the folklore behind it is fascinating. I used to love your grandmother's ghost stories as a kid, even if I never believed them. That's why I gave you the book."

My mind conjured up the image of the Japanese folklore book he'd given me as a teenager. I'd always thought it odd coming from a guy who preferred the news over a novel. In this new light, the gift suddenly made more sense. Dad was giving me a piece of my grandmother's beliefs. Just like we bought *omamori*, little blessed trinkets made of fabric sold at Shinto shrines, he didn't actually believe they held any extra luck. He just liked their connection to his heritage.

I, on the other hand, had a lot more personally invested in these family tales. "Anything else you know about Fumiko?"

"Nothing that immediately comes to mind." Dad glanced at the microwave clock. "I need to get going. Are you sure you can't stay tonight and see your mother?"

"Sorry, but I can't. I've got stuff to do."

He picked up the briefcase. "Then call her when you get a chance. She worries about you. And you'll lock up when you leave?"

"Of course." I gave him a quick hug. He patted me lightly on the back, not much for physical affection, but I recognized the warmth in his eyes as he pulled away.

"Take care, Imogene," he said softly, then headed out the garage door.

I waited until I heard his car pull out of the driveway before I blew out a long breath. So, my great aunt was supposedly possessed by a lightning fox in Japan. Did that mean she'd encountered a fox dryant? I pulled out my phone and did a quick search on ninko but didn't find much more than what Dad had already told me.

The only other thing I could think to do was find that old folklore book. It still rested on my bedroom shelf, shoved between graphic novels and a college math textbook I couldn't sell back my freshman year. Skimming through the section on kitsune only provided a few extra details: how foxes and humans lived in harmony in ancient Japan, that the number of tails the fox had hinted at their strength, and their various abilities ranged from everything to fire and lightning to human possession and invisibility. It all sounded too fantastical, even for me.

I replaced the book on the shelf, wondering if whatever happened to Aunt Fumiko had anything to do with me now. She sounded like she at least had ken like Vincent's family.

In the end, none of this did me any good. I'd accomplished what I came for: grabbing the credit card. It would ease my mom's worry and grant me extra purchasing power in a pinch. I pushed all family stories aside, telling myself to feel grateful for that.

CHAPTER 10

BY THE TIME I trudged my weary carcass back to Sipho's homestead, I was crispy done. My limbs had stiffened from walking in the forest all day, I'd become too tired to regulate my body temperature with sigils, so my sweaty clothes stuck to my skin, and I had a head full of competing thoughts that threatened to topple me at any moment. Even in the dimming light, I must have looked like a hot mess because Callum gasped as I shambled near the vegetable garden.

"Yikes. What happened to you?"

"Life." I watched him rub his lower back. "Tough work, huh?"

He wrinkled his nose. "Ugh. I'd be happy to eat dirt right now if it meant I never dug up another root vegetable again."

"How'd your shopping trip last night go?"

He wrinkled his nose. "I wandered around downtown Eugene for three hours. Epic fail. Nothing felt right."

"Sorry, kid. At least you tried." I glanced around the quiet meadow leading toward the cluster of buildings in the distance. "Who's all here?"

"Guntram just left to relieve Baot. I also saw—"

A sudden primal shriek cut into our conversation, echoing twice before fading away. Somewhere in its vicinity, a thin column of flame launched itself skyward. It exploded into a whirlwind of flame, the sparks falling back toward the creek side of the homestead.

"—Azar," Callum finished lamely.

"I can see that."

Callum leaned against his enchanted hoe for support. "She's been like that all day. She looks even worse than you, if you can believe it."

So much for calm, cool Azar. "She's had a rough day. Let her blow off some steam."

"I guess we're all dead tired." Callum wiped his brow. "What I wouldn't give for a soda."

"You mean a pop?"

"No, they're called 'sodas.'"

Uncultured swine. "Why didn't you buy one yesterday?"

"I dunno."

Actually, now that he mentioned it, a sugary drink would really hit the spot. Pulling water out of the air quenched a shepherd's thirst, but it was hardly satisfying. "Why don't we go get some now then? My treat."

"Really?" Callum leaned forward eagerly. "Nah, I can't waste your hard-earned cash."

I whipped out my mother's new credit card. "Don't worry. I got us covered with this."

I couldn't have enthralled the teen more if I'd flashed him the Holy Grail. "What? No way! Where'd you get that?"

I tapped the card against a temple. "I've got responsible parents back in the 'burbs. They sometimes take pity on me and give me a card to make sure I'm doing okay."

Callum's smile faltered. "Must be nice."

"I know, right? I can buy candy bars, get fast food—"

"I mean having loving parents."

Oof. Despite all my grumbling, I really was lucky to

have my mom and dad in my life. They might not understand me, but they certainly supported me. Callum had grown up neglected and alone. My normal upbringing was a dream by comparison.

I threw my arm around his shoulders. "I'm like a genie in a lamp. Tell me three things you could eat right now, and we can go buy 'em."

"I probably got other stuff to do," he grumbled, a dark cloud still over his head.

"By my calculations, Sipho probably also needs batteries for her headphones. Remember what happened the last time she ran out?"

Callum shuddered involuntarily. "Yeah, but won't we be gone too long?"

"I know a convenience store about a fifteen-minute walk from here. It's got a limited selection, but if you're craving carbonated beverages, you're bound to find something."

The hint of a grin slid on his lips despite him trying to brood. "I guess it couldn't hurt."

"That's the spirit!" I slapped him on the back. "Now c'mon before I change my mind and fix you a garden salad for dinner."

* * *

I got a little teary-eyed as we approached Carol and Dennis's store. It's crazy to get sentimental over a badly aging highway pit stop, but I'd really missed the place with its advertising signage from the 80s. This had been my only connection to my old life for months after I accepted the call to become a shepherd of Nasci. Guntram had rarely let me out of his sight, but I could go for walks on my own. Snarfing down an occasional bag of chips or helping Carol with sudoku made the transition from college student to nature wizard a little easier. A home away from home.

I led Callum across the unpaved parking lot. He nearly tripped on a large pothole not far from the front entrance. "You wanna go in here?"

I scowled at the hole. I'm pretty sure that was a relic of my little run-in with Darby. "It's cleaner inside than outside. Trust me."

Callum sighed as I pushed the streaked glass door open, but he did follow.

Carol glanced up from her folded puzzle book and beamed. "Ina! I was worried you wouldn't take us up on our offer."

"And I brought a friend." I stepped aside to shove the suddenly shy teenager forward. "Meet Callum."

Carol frowned. "He looks a little young for you, dear."

I snort-laughed at that unexpected statement. Callum made a strangling noise in the back of his throat. He would have bolted if I hadn't grabbed him by the elbow.

I made up a lie on the spot. "We're not dating. He's my chem lab partner."

"Is that so?" Carol squinted at Callum.

Callum squirmed.

I laughed, the sound loud in my ears. "He graduated high school early. Callum loves to hike like me. I thought I'd show him some of my favorite trails."

To my relief, Carol accepted this explanation. "It's good you have a buddy out there. Can't be too careful." She waved us off toward the refrigerated shelves at the back of the store. "Help yourself, although Dennis made me promise not to let you drink us out of business."

Good ol' cranky Dennis. He'd given me free stuff before, but he made a fuss when Carol did it. So typical. "Thanks. I'll take the one bottle on the house, but everything else I can buy myself."

Callum waited until Carol's attention returned to scribbling in her book before pulling me down an aisle where she couldn't see us. "What's the deal? I'm not some child genius."

"We needed a cover story. She got suspicious of me too at first when I started showing up regularly. They know I don't live in the area, so I told them I was a local college student."

"But why drag me into it?"

"It'll give you an excuse too." I pulled the nearest bag of chips off the shelf and shoved it into his face. "Don't you like cheesy puffs?"

He pushed them aside. "I'm more of a sour cream chip guy myself." He tried to smoothly snatch a green bag next to my shoulder, but instead knocked it to the ground. Blushing, he scrambled to pick them up.

I stifled a giggle. "Good luck with all that. I'm gonna go pick up my pop." I popped the last 'p' for emphasis, which caused him to grumble even more.

I took my time savoring my selection, wavering over delicious artificial flavors. While I thralled with indecision, Callum grabbed the most neon green beverage out of the refrigerator.

"Really? You're one of those types?"

Callum tapped the can on his forehead. "We're followers of Nasci, Ina. We do the dew."

Outwardly I groaned, but inside, he earned some legit pun cred with me.

I picked out a cherry cola and wandered over to the dustiest shelf in the far back of the store, where Carol and Dennis displayed all the non-perishables. The area held an air of neglect. Most customers bought food and drinks at the store. The anemic stock of random household and camping supplies hadn't been touched for ages except for two items: the AA batteries (which I'd been buying in bulk since last summer) and a couple flat red plastic packages with black pull straps.

I picked up one of these new curious items, reading the label. "What's with the fire blankets?" I called out to Carol.

"Been a lot more wildfires in recent years," she hollered back. "Can't be too careful."

It made sense in an unfortunate way. Humans had mismanaged the forests so long, even the shepherds noticed the increasingly uncontrollable forest fires. Fires are part of the circle of life for many trees. If you repress fire too long in a forest, it can create pure utter destruction over hundreds of thousands of acres not intended by Mother Nature.

I leaned forward to put the fire blanket back when Callum suddenly grabbed me by the wrist. I let out an involuntary yelp.

"What's the deal?"

He ignored me, ripping the fire blanket out of my grasp. He held it with both palms like a scholar might handle a precious book. He held his pop can in the crook of his elbow, where it slowly slipped out of his grasp. I caught it before it hit the floor.

Callum didn't even notice. "This is it! The material for the ward."

I shifted my hoodie sleeves so the two beverages wouldn't give me freezer burn. "Are you sure?"

He nodded so enthusiastically, I worried his head might twist off around his oversized Adam's apple. "I don't know how to explain it, but it feels perfect."

I read over his shoulder dubiously. "It says it's made of fiberglass. Shouldn't you be looking for something more natural?"

"It puts out fires, and isn't magma really just a version of fire?"

"No, it's not."

Callum wasn't deterred. "You gotta buy this. I won't know for sure until I test it with the lesion dirt."

I glanced at the price tag and sighed. Fifty bucks, probably marked way up than if we bought it elsewhere. But we didn't have a lot of time to price shop.

"You still got the cash I gave you?"

Callum patted his shirt pocket. "Yeah."

At least I could use the rest of my cash for this so Mom

wouldn't freak out. I hadn't meant to spend more than a few bucks. "Fine," I said, gesturing him toward the front counter. "Let's buy this stuff and get out of here before you ask for something else."

He beamed at me, happy as any toddler who's successfully wrangled his parent into buying a piece of junk toy. And to be clear, that's really what I thought the fire blanket was. There were all sorts of warnings on the package about how it could "only be used for small fires" and "be careful with fiberglass fragments" and oh by the way, "it irritates people's skin." I kind of doubted it could be used for a ward, but who was I to crush the poor kid's soul?

Better let experience do that for him instead.

Callum snatched the fire blanket after we paid cash for it and hid outside while I bought the food and drinks. It always took a while for Carol's squirrel-based internet connection to run credit cards.

While we waited, Carol announced, "Just so you know, I'm still rooting for that park ranger who was fond of you. You seen him lately?"

My stomach clenched. "No. We had a falling out."

"Ah, now that's too bad." She had me sign the receipt. "He seemed like such a nice guy when he dropped packages off for you. Like he really cared about you."

"He sure did seem liked he cared," I managed, then I too hightailed it outside. Much as I waxed nostalgic about the store, I could have lived without those particular memories.

CHAPTER 11

I LEFT CALLUM skipping off to the forge with his new toy. I looked around the homestead, but even Azar had taken her fiery frustration to bed with her. I took a nice long soak in the hot spring and then got some sleep myself.

The incessant cawing of ravens woke me up as light brightened the morning sky. I pulled the blanket over my head to ignore them, but even if I had succeeded (I didn't), Guntram's loud pounding at my door secured my fate.

"Wake up, Ina. You're on guard duty at Noti."

Grumpy and bleary-eyed, I dragged my butt to the lodge kitchen to find Guntram steeping a pot of tea. "You're late."

I stretched my arms as far as they would allow. "Have you checked the time? You're early."

Guntram poured himself a cup. "You were supposed to relieve me an hour ago. I had to leave Fechin and a few scouts to keep watch."

"Don't get your cloak all up in a twist. Just give me long enough to have breakfast, and I'll be outta here." I gestured toward his kettle. "Can I have some?"

"Sure, as long as you don't befoul it with multiple

spoonfuls of honey."

"Ha. Ha." I took great pleasure staring at him while I did just that.

He grumbled but settled in on his tea.

I missed these quiet moments with my mentor. I'd been so annoyed with being joined at the hip with him as his eyas, I didn't realize how much I'd miss the banter now that I'd graduated a level. He may have been a stubborn, cranky old guy, but he really cared about me, even though I often flung his own hard-earned advice back in his face.

I let my hands warm around the lopsided homemade mug. "Any word on your duel with Sertalis?"

"It's only been a day. Have patience."

I tried to keep the whine out of my voice, but I didn't have the strength this early in the morning. "I hate waiting. It's the worst."

"There are many things worse than waiting."

"Like what?"

"We could have to deal with the vaettur to the north."

I snorted. "You're not going to make me feel sorry for those guys. Let them run after their little vaettur. I hope it takes a chunk out of Sertalis."

A sudden wind blew through the air. Guntram slammed his cup on the counter, his shoulders stiff and back arched. "You do not mean that!"

His sudden attitude adjustment made me flinch. I raised my hands in surrender. "Whoa, sorry. Didn't mean to touch a nerve."

Guntram shrank a little. "I suppose you don't know."

Well that sounded ominous. "Know what?"

"The Oracle sent me a blue jay early this morning. They've identified the vaettur. It's a fenrir."

I paused with the mug halfway to my mouth. Fenrirs are the boogey monsters of the shepherd world. Huge, fast, monstrous wolves that fought more physically than magically, making them hard to banish. They had a decent kill ratio with shepherds, often requiring a coordinated group to take down for safety.

A flash of smug relief came over me. Let the arrogant jerks in the north deal with it.

Then I felt guilty for having such an ugly thought. "Should we go help them?"

"I sent a raven as an offer, but I doubt they will accept."

My jaw clenched in anger. "They believe they're better than us."

"We have our own problems. With a fenrir running loose in the north, our race to seal the lesion becomes even more desperate. I shudder to think what powers a fenrir would receive if it drank Nasci's lifeblood."

A sizzle went up my own spine. A few weeks ago, a vaettur swarm of locusts had found the lesions. They'd become more aggressive and powerful, becoming very difficult to banish. And the chumal were considered moderate-level vaetturs, not a heavyweight like a fenrir.

Guntram must have understood my terror because he reached over to pat my arm. "Do not worry. The last fenrir sighting occurred in Colville National Forest, several hundred miles from here."

He had meant to calm me, but he'd done the opposite. I sprang to my feet. "I thought I heard at the meeting that the vaettur had been in the Okanogan area."

Guntram drew back in surprise. "Those were the original sightings yes, but the fenrir was spotted yesterday in Colville. Why does that bother you?"

Because I knew of one other person who had gone wolf hunting in Colville: Vincent Garcia.

I forced myself to breathe before I passed out. I needed some logic to calm down. Vaetturs rarely attacked normal people. Vanilla humans didn't have enough juicy pith worth devouring. Of course, Vincent had some ken, but not like a shepherd. He was probably fine. And, of course, the Colville National Forest was a huge area. Odds were good he was safe.

Guntram kept his worried eyes on me. "Ina?"

But I had to be sure. "Tell me the fenrir was nowhere near Trout Creek."

For a heartbeat, I honestly believed everything would work out. Guntram would assure me the fenrir was nowhere in that particular neck of the woods. I could text Vincent to warn him of the danger, and if I had to, I could go find him and haul him out of the area myself.

But instead, Guntram's mouth fell open a little. "Yes, near where it meets Sherman Creek. How did you know?"

Dread washed over me. Too many coincidences were lining up. And they all pointed to my ex-boyfriend wandering around by himself with one of the toughest creatures of Letum stalking him.

I knocked over one of the counter stools in my scramble for the front door. "Get someone else to take my shift!" I yelled over my shoulder.

"Ina?" Guntram's voice rang in my ears as I fled as fast as my feet could carry me across the meadow. "Ina! Stop!"

But I didn't stop. I wouldn't stop. I had to find Vincent before it was too late.

CHAPTER 12

THICK TRUNKS AND scraggly branches whizzed by in a hazy blur as I dashed my way north through miles of dense forest. I took the most direct route to Colville National Forest, through mountainsides that required earth pith to navigate steep terrain. My calves and glutes screamed in agony as I plunged through wisp channel after wisp channel. I pushed it all aside to focus on one single goal.

Finding Vincent before the fenrir.

About halfway to Colville I caught a lucky break through an even meadow: strong cellphone service. I hit Vincent's contact info. The phone slapped against my ear as I ran. The call went straight to voicemail. Vincent had probably turned off his phone to conserve power.

My brain attempted to calm me down. Maybe a fenrir hadn't killed Christy's uncle. Maybe Vincent would get even more mad at me for showing up unannounced. Maybe I was overreacting.

But I somehow knew the clock was ticking. I've never claimed to have any sort of sixth sense about anything. I'm the kind of person who walks down a street and barely notices the people walking past me. And yet I knew something was horribly wrong, and if I didn't get to Vincent soon, I'd regret it for the rest of my life.

I jumped out of a wisp channel where the mouth of Sherman Creek met the Columbia River. The creek would eventually meet up with Trout Creek, so I followed its meandering banks west. It paralleled a rural highway. Pine trees clustered along the southern shoulder. I jogged along the high ground, watching vehicles flash by like mini shooting stars below. After a decent distance, I noticed a narrow road branching north from the highway. I almost passed it but noticed a bent sign with the words "Trout Lake Road."

Bingo. I scrambled down to the guardrail, waiting until the coast was clear before zipping across the highway. This new road, although public, was made of dirt. I immediately found the creek that bore the lake's name. Sweaty and tired, I slowed my pace, allowing me to catch my breath.

Despite arriving at my destination, the remaining hundred or so square miles around the creek still resulted in a saguaro needle-in-the-desert search. Vincent could be anywhere around here. I focused most of my attention on Trout Creek itself. I hoped to catch a glimpse of a campsite or vehicle tracks leading back into the woods.

What I didn't expect was a steady wail.

It started as a low-pitched hum, the kind of buzz you ignore because you just want it to go away. But as I drew closer, it grew in intensity, a sustained note of doom. It took me a while to figure out what it was, but when I did, my heart went cold.

It was an uninterrupted car horn.

I swiveled my head from right to left, pinpointing the source in a slightly southern direction. I sprinted up a hill, ending at the top of a small ridge.

I spotted the illegal campsite right away. It was the perfect hidden location on the opposite side of the hill where no one would spot it from the road. It also had water access next to Trout Creek. A sagging canvas tent and decades-old pickup truck squatted together next to discarded tools and a fire pit with recent ashes.

But it wasn't the pickup making the noise. The horn emitted from somewhere in the trees. And a trail of what appeared to be blood led toward that ominous blare. Straight out of a slasher film.

I gulped, clenching my defensive charm in my right hand as I skidded down to the campsite. I gave the area a quick glance as I slunk past but noted nothing unusual. Then I faced the real menace, following the awful red trail as the trees crowded in around me.

My mouth went bone dry as I scanned the foliage around me. The density of the brush made it almost impossible to see farther than a few feet. I squeezed the lightning charm with my free left hand, letting its erratic energy sizzle. I wavered between concentrating on defensive versus offensive magic. A fenrir might have the raw physical strength to snap my defensive charm in two with one bite, but then again, I might not have time to pull off even a lightning sigil if it attacked at close range.

A sudden scurry of gray fur on the path ahead almost gave me a heart attack. I recognized it as a squirrel with whole nanoseconds to spare. The poor thing had no idea how close it had become to getting fried.

The trees abruptly thinned, and a familiar silver Subaru came into view. Something had created jagged tears along the body and slashed its tires. The blood trail led directly to the driver's side door with matching smears around the handle. But the real nightmare fuel was a shadowy figure that lay slumped against the steering wheel, unmoving.

"Vincent!" I yelled as I crossed the last few yards between us.

I didn't make it.

Something slammed into my side without warning. It's a good thing I still had a grip on both charms because they went off simultaneously, saving my life. The defensive charm prevented a savage rake of teeth from clamping down on my midsection. My left pinkie managed a quick zigzag, and the lightning charm exploded in sparks, sending my attacker and me flying in opposite directions. I ping-ponged off a nearby tree before landing in a heap on the ground.

Everything hurt as the blinding light receded. I placed a palm on the ground to stand, but stabbing pains slid me back to the ground. The defensive charm had shattered in my hand, and two sharp metal shards had embedded in the sensitive flesh.

I wobbled upright using my non-dominant hand and scanned for my assailant. I couldn't see anything but scorched earth and burning reeds.

A howl cut through the air like a knife.

The still-blaring car horn should have made it impossible to hear, but that only tells you how incredibly loud a fenrir howl is. Survival instincts told me to move, stat. I half stumbled, half lumbered over to the silver Subaru, too dizzy to walk in a straight line.

I jerked on the backseat door handle, stunned to find it locked. "You've got to be kidding me."

The horn abruptly silenced, filling the air with a sustained growl. On the other side of the car, in the gloom of the forest canopy, a hulking shadow shifted toward me. I live in the forest, so I'm used to the scale of larger land mammals. The size of elk, moose, and even bears doesn't intimidate me. But this beast was at least one and a half times larger than any of those animals.

There's a reason why wolves are engrained in our culture. From fairy tales to bad teenage romance books, they are the true stuff of nightmares. This vaettur version had metallic-colored fur like the Subaru, reflecting the light where it broke through the leaves. Highlights of blue fur were woven in a latticework-type pattern, blinking with its own lights like dying Christmas lights left on random repeat. The fenrir's monstrous yellow eyes fixed on me, lips curled back in a snarl to expose a double set of sharp canines, eight in all.

And with a powerful spring of its back legs, it bounded toward me.

I screamed like girls always do in horror movies, shrill and high. I'd never made that sound before, and I doubted I could repeat it on command.

"Ina!" A muffled cry issued from within the car, then the distinct click of an unlocking door. "Get in!"

I scrambled inside, pulling my legs in as the fenrir sprang over the hood. I slammed the door shut as claws raked where I had just been standing. Frustrated at its loss, the wolf flung its massive front paws at the car, rocking the vehicle violently back and forth.

I squealed, scooting to the other side of the car to create the illusion of more safe space between us.

The fenrir coiled backward to launch a second attack at the window. I thought we were dead until Vincent jammed his fist back on the car horn, slicing the environment with its awful racket. The wolf howled in return, slinking back into the thick brush. Its weird glowing patterns faded into the shadows as if someone had unplugged their power source. Vincent kept up the car horn until it was well out of sight before finally letting go.

Vincent wheezed as he turned around to face me. "Are you...okay?"

I panted as the noise drained from my ears, attempting to get oxygen circulating in my panic-riddled body. I finally got a good look at him. The fenrir may have knocked the wind out of me, but Vincent's condition took my breath away. Cuts and bruises lined his face, scars from a recent scuffle. He was bare chested, streaks of blood and dirt on his arms and torso, although the wounds all seemed superficial.

"Vince! What happened?"

"The wolf jumped me." Vincent took an unsteady breath. "If I hadn't had this, I'd be dead." He unraveled the fingers of his fist to show me two pieces of a thin slat of metal similar to the one I'd blasted apart in my hand.

"The defensive charm I gave you last month?"

Vincent nodded. "I'd forgotten all about it until the wolf bit me. It couldn't penetrate my skin the first few times it tried. I couldn't figure it out until I remembered you'd given me this."

I let out a breath. "So the charm saved you."

He winced and clenched his right leg. "I wouldn't go that far."

I leaned over the center console and discovered why he'd removed his shirt. He'd wrapped it around his thigh in a tourniquet, blood soaking through the navy fabric.

I inhaled a sharp, whistling breath.

"Yeah," Vincent agreed. "But I would have been wolf meat three times over without your charm. It at least kept me alive."

"I'm glad you didn't cut yourself on the shards." I lifted my punctured hand to show him my gory palm.

Vincent swore. "You need to clean that and wrap it."

"I'll live. You might not." I bit my lower lip so hard, I'm surprised I didn't draw more blood. "We need to get you to a hospital."

"I tried. The wolf attacked the car as soon as it started moving." He pointed toward the battered hood. "It won't run now."

"What about calling for help?"

"I'm not getting any bars out here."

I checked my phone. Same thing. My mind scrambled for another solution. "Maybe that pickup back at the camp runs."

"Even if it does, we can't get to it from here. The wolf will attack us."

As if on cue, the wolf flung itself into the glass next to my head, causing a hairline crack. I jumped so high, I hit my head on the roof of the car.

Then Vincent did something I'd only seen him do once before. He held one palm out toward the thrashing fenrir and squinted his eyes in concentration. Incredibly, the fenrir froze as if playing a magical game of Red Light, Green Light, its limbs bent at unnatural angles since it had been swiping at the car. It snarled as it fell over as stiff as a board, gravity pulling it down.

Once the fenrir could not so much as twitch, Vincent released his hold and slammed the car horn again. I plugged one ear with my uninjured hand and pressed the other against the passenger seat's fabric to drown the noise. The beast howled as it scrambled back to its feet. Spittle flying from its canines, it fled back into the dark.

Vincent collapsed back in his seat. "It's the only thing I've figured that drives it away."

I shakily removed my finger. "D-Did you just freeze the fenrir? With pith?"

"Yeah," he said between huge gulps of breath. "I guess I owe you an apology."

He'd frozen a vaettur once before to save me. Outrage overcame the fear of the situation. "Are you telling me you could use magic this whole time?"

"No. I mean yes. Ah, hell." He sat up straighter and willed himself to focus on me. "Look, things are nuts. I got attacked by a giant wolf and realized I had this...this ability."

"You mean the magic you insisted you don't have?"

He swallowed hard. "I've had a few hours to think while slowly bleeding out. I was stubborn and completely wrong. You were right about me having magic. I just didn't want to admit it."

"And what about your mom? Aren't you still mad about me crashing the family's cozy little get together?"

He grew paler by the minute. "No. Oscar invited you. And it wasn't your fault my mom treated you like dirt. She's always like that with people she considers 'outsiders.' I should have taken your side."

"Well, isn't that convenient?" I threw my hands up in the air. "You had an epiphany out here in the woods.

Should I give you a cookie?"

But then he reached out to touch a tendril of hair that had fallen in my face. "I'm sorry, Ina. I've been a real jerk. You don't have to accept anything I have to offer you."

A lump formed in my throat, my anger vanishing. "I'm just happy you're okay. We'll figure this out."

He didn't say anything, just kept stroking my hair. I leaned into it, content to sit there with him. Even in the middle of this disaster, a weight lifted off my shoulders. If Vincent was with me, it didn't matter how bad things got. We could handle anything.

Then his hand pulled back. That alone wouldn't have been cause for alarm, except his head also lolled over to one side.

Vincent had passed out.

CHAPTER 13

"VINCENT?" I ASKED, panic rising in my voice. I shoved him with my good hand. "Hey, wake up!"

Vincent fell over in an awkward position with his temple against the driver's side window.

"Oh no." I scrambled to get closer to him. "No, no, no." I drew a sigil and splashed some water on his face, but to no avail. He'd gone completely limp. If I hadn't noticed him breathing, I might have had a full nervous breakdown right there.

But Vincent was still alive. He needed me to get him through this.

Something moved outside the window. I caught a glimpse of a bushy tail behind a thorny bush. My choices were limited. Staying would ensure Vincent's death. I could try dragging Vincent to the pickup, but that would take a ton of earth sigils and expose both of us to attack. If I escaped the fenrir by myself to call for help, there was no telling if Vincent would survive. Even if I did manage to call an ambulance, the EMTs couldn't see the monster in the woods. Would it attack and kill them too?

That left me with one gut-wrenching (and potentially gut-spilling) option: to take down the fenrir myself.

I grabbed onto my lightning charm with my right hand out of instinct, hissing as the embedded shards dug deeper into the skin. I yanked them out and then pulled my hoodie sleeve over the palm. Take down a boss-level vaettur with an injured dominant drawing hand. Sure. No problem.

But then Vincent rasped while unconscious. What choice did I have?

I brushed my fingers against the lightning charm again. Not surprisingly, I'd used up all its juice. That left me with the standard elements at my disposal. How had Tabitha taken a fenrir down by herself? She'd been an earth augur, so it made sense she'd use that element as her primary weapon. I definitely didn't have the chops to pull off any spectacular earth sigils. It wasn't exactly my strongest skill.

But then I thought of what I could do with earth. Maybe I had a chance after all. I pooled heavy earth pith in my forearms and exited the car.

When you know the worst is coming, you want to get it over with. It's like going to the doctor's office for a blood withdrawal. I hate the anticipation with all the rubber bands and alcohol swabs. Just stick me with the damn needle and get it over with already.

Apparently the fenrir didn't get the memo because I did two full circles around the car without observing its ugly mug.

"Hey, Fangface!" I called. "Come get me!"

Nothing howled back.

I grimaced. Vincent had parked the Subaru on a relatively flat field, but I was hemmed in by dense trees. I needed to draw the fenrir out into a more open area. That meant doubling back to the camp, through trees that could hide the fenrir.

Shaking with nervous jitters, I headed in that direction.

I scanned the encroaching foliage for any sign of movement. I swear I could feel every nerve ending in my body, screaming for me to take cover. Not even the wind stirred around me, the leaves as still as if painted on branches. The very atmosphere held its breath as it waited to see the consequences of my stupidity for baiting a legendary wolf monster. I glanced behind me, but the Subaru had already vanished behind a wall of forest.

Then two things happened back-to-back.

First, a cacophony of caws broke out to my left, accompanied by a swarm of black feathers flapping into the sky. I slid into a sigil stance toward them out of habit.

And second, perhaps triggered by the ravens or my momentary distraction, the fenrir lunged toward me.

Scrambling backwards, I drew squares within squares within squares, flinging earth pith where I had stood moments ago. I had mere seconds for my frantic idea to work, and if I failed, I wouldn't even get a snarky comment in edgewise before the wolf ate me faster than Red Riding Hood's grandma.

The ground cracked apart like a giant gaping mouth, complete with jagged edges. The fenrir, aiming for my throat, had committed to a trajectory that hinged on me being where I'd created the hole. I wrote one last square with a looping line, and the dirt beneath my boots pushed me even farther away, out of the fenrir's impressive reach.

The fenrir went down, down, down into empty space. We locked eyes as gravity took hold. It swiped one mighty paw but only batted empty air between us.

Then it fell out of sight.

I didn't waste any time with the follow through. I grabbed the earth charm for surplus pith, ignoring the pain in my good hand as I wrote sigils to close the pit over the wolf. The sides of the crater collapsed back in on itself, filling up like a pitcher of water overturned into a sink. I wrote squares like mad, frantic to bury the vaettur before it could tear loose.

And then the hole closed. Besides upturned weeds crisscrossing the spot, the circular patch of dirt actually looked pretty normal for the middle of the woods. I

90

collapsed on my butt, more from sheer terror than exertion. I waited for the ground to stir and indicate the fenrir was climbing back out, but nothing happened.

"I did it," I whispered.

I hadn't banished the wolf, merely trapped it. You can't kill creatures of Letum outright, only banish them back to their world, but I didn't have that kind of mojo right now. The wolf would remain down there until shepherds finished the job.

But I sighed in relief, knowing I'd at least bought some time. I took a step back toward Vincent.

My former crater exploded with the force of a live grenade.

The blast thrust me onto my hands and knees, plant detritus coating the inside of my surprised mouth. I twisted around to watch the fenrir leaping toward me in an arc, the lattice patterns on its back glowing so bright it made the wolf seem more like a specter than an animal. Its yellow eyes also glowed with rage as it plunged downward, jaws snapping.

I guess if this had to be my last sight on Earth, at least it looked cool.

Except I didn't die. A gale force wind slammed into the fenrir, knocking it off course. The vaettur smacked straight into a thorny blackberry bush, howling.

"INA!" Guntram's voice stabbed my mental fog. "MOVE!"

I staggered to my feet and ran back down the tire ruts, away from the vaettur. Guntram emerged under a cloud of squawking feathers to join me in my mad dash.

"Have you lost your mind?" he demanded. "Running to take on a fenrir by yourself?"

"I came to find Vincent!" I yelled back. "I knew he was out here in the woods."

"You should have let the north handle it!"

Adrenaline fueled my anger. "You should have banished the wolf!"

Guntram gave me a glare that could melt steel. "What do you think I was trying to do back there?"

If Guntram had hit the fenrir dead on with a powerful air sigil backed by a five-pointed star, and the fenrir survived, we were truly screwed.

Guntram grabbed my arm to increase my pace. "A fenrir is dangerous because it relies on physical force and speed rather than magic. It has no particular elemental vulnerabilities, making it difficult to effectively attack. You have to hit it with enough banishment force and hope for the best. Even so, it doesn't always work. The fenrir may create a new breach and slink back to Letum to lick its wounds."

I winced at that last point. It takes serious mojo to create one breach between Letum and Nasci. I'd never heard of a vaettur able to create a second one, and on Earth no less.

Still, I recognized a potential silver lining. I yanked myself out of his grasp. "Let's just throw everything we've got at it and hope it goes away."

"It's not that simple. A fenrir will always return if you don't banish it, sometimes within hours. And it generally becomes more ferocious than before."

Fantastic, a vaettur with a grudge. "Well, we don't have a lot of options right now. I gotta draw the fenrir away from the vehicle. Vincent's hurt and needs help now."

"We don't have time. We require backup, the sooner the better. I already sent a raven to—"

The rest of Guntram's message got lost in a fierce flurry of raven caws as the fenrir knocked him over. The combined mass of augur and vaettur missed me by inches as they skidded behind me.

"Guntram!" I ground to a halt, hands up to draw as I turned to attack.

Only they were already on the move. Guntram had zipped upward in a burst of air. The fenrir freaking leaped after him. The wolf got in a blow that glanced off

Guntram's defensive sigil, throwing him back toward the ground.

What happened next, I could barely track due to the sheer speed of the two opponents. Guntram and the fenrir squared off, the air augur blasting wind toward the wolf wherever he could get a shot, keeping the wolf out of biting range. Undeterred, the wolf used trunks and rocks to hide before rebounding against the vulnerable shepherd. Guntram added bits of earth blasts and fireballs to his volleys, but the fenrir avoided them all. They zigzagged in a flurry of dodges, neither one gaining much ground as they fled farther into the woods. I tried to write sigils to help Guntram, but I couldn't finish any fast enough. Before long, the fight had already moved on elsewhere.

Guntram desperately needed support, but I wasn't helping.

"C'mon, Ina. Do something." I wished my lightning charm wasn't drained. I glanced around me for inspiration. We'd circled back to the silver Subaru.

Maybe I could get a refill from the car's battery.

Before I could implement my new plan, however, a pained cry filled the air. I couldn't see Guntram, but his kidamas' racket rose to a fever pitch.

"Guntram!" There was no time for fancy plans. I changed course back into the woods.

A sudden wave of heat hit me first. It rolled over me like a blanket, accompanied by a thick plume of smoke. I coughed, waving my hands in front of my sore eyes until flickers of light penetrated my vision.

The forest had suddenly caught fire.

An approaching snarl caught my attention down the path. The fenrir rushed out of the trees yards ahead, bits of ash flying off its illuminated fur. It paused to curl one lip at me, blood dripping from its mouth. A predator's gaze, considering if I was worth the effort.

Then a fireball nearly clocked it on the head. The fenrir yipped, skirting to one side as the ground melted to blackened ash where it had stood. It zipped back into a grove of trees, retreating away from a second volley of heavenly fire.

I drew the walking in fire sigil and then stood my ground between the burning trees and the silver Subaru, determined to keep Vincent safe from magical attacks. "The fenrir's gone!" I screamed to be heard above the sudden roar. "Ax the fire before you hurt someone!"

I wasn't certain anyone heard me until the flames suddenly winked out of existence. I blinked in confusion at the singed plants, tall and wide, surrounding me. Even Azar needed more time to douse that many flames. She couldn't turn them on and off like a light bulb.

The outline of a person emerged in the smoky haze, heading toward me. "Working on your fire skills?" I called out. "You've been holding out on me, Guntram."

"You think the old windbag could do that?" Sertalis dove out of the smoke, a handful of garter snakes slithering at his feet. He looked every bit an angry demon, flames flickering over his dark clothes and giving him an orange glow.

I gaped. "What are you doing here?"

Sertalis shook himself and the flames on him just disappeared. "That should be my question to you, lightning shepherd." He spat the world 'lightning' out like a curse.

This was my first real glimpse of what Sertalis could do with fire. I'd be lying if I said it didn't scare me a little. "I...I..."

"We are all Talol Wilds shepherds, Sertalis," a serene voice answered from behind him.

"Oracle?" Sertalis backed away from me, obviously surprised as another figure emerged, supporting a limping third shepherd. Despite their size difference, the Oracle did not appear winded (pun intended) by supporting a grimacing Guntram on her shoulder.

"I wisped here from Okanogan as soon as Fechin

located me," she declared. "But it appears I missed our foe."

Sertalis nodded. "I was on patrol in the area and heard the ravens. It is as you suspected. The fenrir has expanded its hunting ground."

Guntram grunted, catching my attention. He appeared mostly okay, except for his right foot, which was coated in so much blood it resembled a dark-colored sock.

I gasped. "Are you okay?"

Guntram gave me a tense smile through his pain. "I'll be fine."

"You were wise to send your kidama for aid," the Oracle told him. "But now you should heal." She faced Sertalis and me. "I will escort him back to the northern homestead. The two of you should pursue the fenrir so we can track its movements."

"I can't," I blurted out.

Sertalis blanched. "You're refusing the Oracle's command?"

I waved toward the Subaru. "There's an injured man in there."

"So?" Sertalis asked.

Guntram gave me a warning stare, but I plunged ahead. "The fenrir attacked him, and he's badly hurt."

For once, the Oracle looked surprised. "The fenrir attacked a regular human? I'm surprised he survived the encounter."

I refused to bring up Vincent's access to a defensive charm, not with Guntram watching me like a hawk, so I merely nodded. "We can save him if we get him to a hospital."

To my dismay, the Oracle hesitated. "If the fenrir attacked one person, it could hurt many others. We need to weigh the consideration of all living things against the well-being of one."

Sertalis snorted. "And what's one less person roaming our woods? Let natural selection take its course. It's what we'd do with any animal."

"We would aid an animal hurt by a creature of Letum," I flung back. Then I turned to the Oracle, not too proud to beg, "You must let me help him."

Her eyebrows shot up with regret, hinting at her answer. I clenched my fists to steady my shaking body. I knew what I had do if she ordered me to leave Vincent to die, but I wasn't excited to get subdued by the most powerful shepherds of the Talol Wilds. Still, I wouldn't abandon Vincent. I mentally calculated how long it would take me to refill my lightning charm with the car battery to have even a fighting chance of winning.

But before the Oracle could say anything, Guntram spoke up. "A vaettur rarely attacks a person without cause. There is probably something more to this man."

"Like what?" Sertalis sneered.

Guntram set his death glare on the fire augur. "Perhaps he has ken like us."

The Oracle frowned in thought.

Sertalis laughed without mirth. "And there it is. Guntram, the would-be savior of haggards everywhere. Would you accept him as an eyas, like your lightning shepherd here?"

Guntram looked like he wanted to brawl with Sertalis despite his maimed foot. "Whether you like to admit it or not, other people have access to Nasci besides shepherds and forgers. Ken doesn't vanish because people aren't trained to use it. In the Onyara Wilds—"

"Spare me the traditions from your wretched homeland," Sertalis interrupted. "If it's so great there, maybe you should return." He added one last line dripping with sarcasm. "I'm sure they'd welcome you back with open arms."

"Enough," the Oracle broke in quietly but with a weight that drove both shepherds off each other. "Go, Ina. See if you can aid this man. Sertalis, track the fenrir if you can. My guess is that it will retreat to Letum, so we should at least seal both its entry and exit breaches. Do not engage, though, if you happen to find it. One shepherd alone cannot defeat it."

Sertalis pursed his lips, obviously upset at her decision, but nodded. Without another glance in our direction, he dove into the forest, his snakes squirming in his wake. The Oracle waved her hand, and a flurry of blue jays I hadn't noticed before followed him.

The Oracle then urged Guntram back into the forest, dismissing me with a wave. I hesitated, knowing how far I'd pushed her already.

"Oracle?" I called after her.

Both Guntram and the Oracle gave me pants-wetting glares.

A nervous titter escaped my lips. "If I could ask for one more teeny, tiny favor?"

CHAPTER 14

YOI WASN'T THE Oracle for nothing.

Using her given name humanized her for me, which was important after witnessing how powerful she really was. I'd asked her for help hauling Vincent from the Subaru to the pickup, knowing I couldn't do it by myself. I expected her to work with me, drawing earth sigils so I could drag him across the ground to the pickup.

But the Oracle did all the heavy lifting for me. With Guntram leaning on her for support, she drew a rapid series of sigils that not only freaking opened the car door (how did she even do that?), but she floated Vincent back to the second vehicle. She weaved her magic so fast I had to sprint in order to open the pickup's passenger door for her. Then she laid him gently inside and even flung some extra pith inside him for good measure. It evened his breathing out a bit. Not a substitute for modern medicine but an appreciated boost nonetheless.

Then, before I could thank her, she disappeared into the forest, hauling a grumpy Guntram with her. Every raven and blue jay for miles swarmed after them.

"I am not worthy," I whispered in her wake. Then I hopped into the pickup's cab, blew a sigh of relief when the keys in the ignition started right away, and drove back to the forest service road.

But with one problem solved, others cropped up. I had no idea where to go for the nearest hospital. Even if I just drove up to it, the situation would raise a lot of questions. At a minimum, I would have to come up with a logical explanation about what happened to Vincent that didn't involve me trying to murder him. I'd seen enough true crime documentaries to know that police interrogation could hold me up for hours, even days. And if a skeptical cop didn't trust me (the random girl with no identification), then I could get charged with who knows what crimes related to Vincent's assault or even the illegal campsite Christy's uncle had made.

My best bet was to find a place to drop Vincent off that would attract help. I pulled over on a wide highway shoulder and pulled out my phone. According to my agonizingly slow map app, Kettle Falls, a burgeoning town of 1,500, was only a ten-minute drive away. I cranked the wheel in that direction.

If you've ever been in an emergency situation, a minute can stretch out into an hour. Although Vincent had looked a lot better after the Oracle's pith injection, his skin had turned as ashen as the pebbles lining the road. Blood stains stood out even more starkly on his arms, resting over his leaking bandage. His increasingly shallow breaths made my heart clench.

I grabbed his floppy hand and squeezed his fingers in mine. "Hang in there, Vince."

As the highway eased out of the mountains toward the Columbia River, dots of civilization finally sprang up around us. I considered turning down any number of gravel driveways to ask for help, but rednecks can be alarmingly vicious. They take their "Trespassers Shot on Sight" signs seriously.

Fortunately, as the signs for Highway 395 became more frequent, so did the industrial buildings. And where there's a lot of fossil-fueled equipment, there's always a gas station, which is exactly what I found at the intersection of the highway and another major road.

To my incredible luck, I hadn't found a Carol and Dennis style place (no offense to my friends) but one of nicer, newer fueling stations. It had a shiny metal roof over the pumps that matched the store's. Five identical blue flags flapped in the breeze to advertise some expensive energy drink. I drove past the nearly empty pumps and parked to the side, far away from the front entrance.

I checked to make sure no one paid me any mind, then I gave Vincent one last squeeze. "Help is on the way," I promised.

Leaving the pickup with Vincent inside, I ducked into a grove of trees that bordered the back, then dialed 9-1-1. I told the operator about spotting a passed-out man in his vehicle that I was worried about. I gave her a description of the truck and name of the gas station, then hung up.

A cop must have been on patrol nearby because he showed up within minutes, making a beeline for the pickup. He hunched over Vincent inside the cab, talking to someone on his shoulder radio. I couldn't hear any specifics given the distance. His actions caught the attention of a store employee, which ushered in a trickle of onlookers, one of which produced a blanket for the police officer.

Then the ambulance came, and everyone stepped back as the EMTs laid Vincent on a stretcher. The police officer took that time to talk to the crowd with a pad of paper and pencil. Everyone shrugged with dumbfounded looks on their faces.

I stuck around until the ambulance pulled away with Vincent inside, lights swirling but with no sirens. I hoped that was a good sign as I sank farther back into the woods. I'd been so absorbed in the drama that I hadn't heard the pair of ravens cawing overhead. They must have followed me on Guntram's orders. They led me to the nearest wisp channel, a good thing since I'd lost my bearings driving around. Shepherds aren't used to navigating via roads.

Leaping through the blue lights to the other side, I recognized my surroundings. I oriented myself toward the Mt. Rainier homestead, hoping things hadn't gone from bad to worse in my short absence.

CHAPTER 15

GOOD OLD OPTIMISTIC me. I love to wish for the impossible and get smacked in the face with reality.

The northern homestead appeared empty at first, the adjacent fields abandoned despite the harvest season. I checked everywhere, hoping to catch a glimpse of Oduvan since she seemed friendly, but no such luck. The Oracle's home also wasn't occupied. Trekking inward, I didn't see anyone around the mountainside buildings either. It was like a repeat of my last visit. I thought for sure I'd find some meeting going on in the amphitheater, yet no one graced its benches.

The only sign of life anywhere was a metal clanging emitting from the forge. I reluctantly headed there. If all the shepherds had left the homestead to search for the fenrir, the forger and her apprentices would stay behind to create items to help with the hunt. That meant my only option to figure out what happened to Guntram was Elif.

That didn't mean I had to like it.

Everything in the northern homestead had been crafted as an architectural masterpiece, and the forge was no exception. Instead of the barnlike structure Sipho built, Elif had constructed a sleek modern fortress out of stone.

It had three rounded concentric shells on the outside, like a warped eco-version of the Sydney Opera House. Two curvy turrets in the corners billowed smoke over their surfaces. Double wooden doors with etched obsidian inlays protected the building from unwanted intruders, preventing anyone without significant pith from passing through. The whole thing looked like a yuppie and a medieval knight co-designed a mansion, and it fit Elif's pretentiousness perfectly.

I made it to within steps of the entrance when a brown mass of fur and claws zipped around a contour of the building. I jumped back as Quavik, the wolverine that guarded the northern homestead, growled at me. He was getting on in years and couldn't have been larger than a golden retriever, but I'd never underestimate this overgrown weasel. I'd heard he'd taken on an alceston, a nasty moose vaettur with wings. He couldn't banish the thing, but he'd supposedly maimed it with his semi-retractable claws and sharp canines.

I stepped back with my hands in the air. "Hey, it's me. A fellow shepherd."

Quavik deepened his snarl. I guess he didn't agree with my assessment.

An airy voice broke into our conversation. "He's as offended by the stink of lesion on you as I am." Elif had quietly opened the forge doorway to peer outside.

I sneered right back at her. "Sorry I haven't had time for a bath. I've been busy."

Elif narrowed her eyes down her nose. "So I've heard. Sertalis has rallied the northern shepherds to clean up your little mess."

"It wasn't my mess. The fenrir attacked inside your territory, not mine."

Elif gave a mirthless laugh. "You think your scent didn't rile the fenrir up?" She leaned over to scratch behind Quavik's ears, who reluctantly settled down, although he kept his focus on me. "Fenrir have superior tracking abilities even above their wolf counterparts. They're clever and can identify that scent."

I stiffened in horror as Elif's words sunk in. The chumal swarm had also sensed the lesions from over a hundred miles away. Could the fenrir do the same?

Elif smirked at my distress. "I see you understand the full scope of our problem."

I straightened my spine. "Where's Guntram? He should know about this."

"Haven't you and your southern shepherds done enough? The northern shepherds have gone to find the fenrir and banish it for good. My apprentices are crafting even as we speak to help them in this task. We have it taken care of."

I wished I could smack her in the jaw, but I forced my hands to stay at my side. "But if it's as bad as you say, you need all the help you can get."

"Your head augur is injured, lounging in our hot spring even as we speak. And besides you, the rest of the south are weak. You're forbidden from facing the fenrir."

"Oh yeah? On whose authority?"

Elif's eyes lit up in what I could only describe as joy. "The Oracle's."

Well, that was a punch to the gut. The Oracle had decided the south should just sit back and play mall cop to the northern shepherd's police task force. I felt physically ill.

Elif waved me off. "Go on now, haggard. Find your augur and put him back in his place guarding his homegrown problems. The real shepherds will handle the rest."

She summoned Quavik inside and shut the door behind her.

It's just as well I hadn't refilled my lightning charm because I might have shattered Elif's stuffy little forge to bits. While it might have given me immense short-term satisfaction, I'd gained the (unfortunate) maturity to know better. I unclenched my jaw as I stalked away to find Guntram.

Unlike the open-air hot spring of the southern homestead, the northern one was located inside Mt. Rainier itself. I walked the rest of the main path until I came to the point where two rocky walls on each side of the little valley met. Before me loomed a massive cave entrance, the source of the mountain spring. I stepped inside, shadows engulfing me at first, but after crunching forward on wet pebbles, the soft glow of torches flickered above me. The cave ceiling sunk as I rounded a corner, the front passageway disappearing behind me and the temperature rising. The spring dove down into some deep rocks I couldn't traverse without sigils, but I followed a narrow branch into a side room with steam rolling out of it like mist.

The hot spring was easily as large as an Olympic swimming pool but never deeper than three feet at any given point. The bumpy volcanic rock of Mt. Rainier created natural seats around its gigantic circumference. More magically lit torches burned underneath the pool's bottom beneath glass cases, lighting up the water so you could view your submerged body. Little alcoves in the walls offered more private areas, like booths in a restaurant, if you wanted to bathe quietly with someone else.

Guntram sat in plain view not far to my right, the only person in the hot spring. His bare shoulders and hairy upper chest indicated he'd stripped naked for his soak, although he'd settled away from a light source, so I didn't have to view his nether regions. It's a good thing too because he'd manspread himself, arms draped over stone like a couch, complete with his head leaned back and his eyes closed. He looked as if he'd fallen asleep after running a marathon.

I didn't want to wake him up if he needed rest, so I quietly backed away. I'd turned my back when his booming voice startled me.

"I'm awake. Come on in."

He didn't have to ask me twice. My poor aching pithways yearned for a dip. Stripping off my clothes and tossing them near Guntram's carefully folded cloak, I eased myself into the stinging waters. We'd seen each other naked plenty of times traveling together in the woods, but even so, I kept my private parts under the water out of modesty. Some habits of civilization die hard.

Instead of staring up Guntram's hairy nostrils, I talked at his shoulder. "Elif says we're supposed to guard the lesions while the northern cavalry takes care of the fenrir without us."

Guntram did not bother to open his eyes or lift his head. "I already knew that."

"You're not upset?"

He gave a half shrug. "It makes sense. We've already split resources in that fashion anyway."

"But you're one of the toughest shepherds in the Talol Wilds. Aren't you mad being put on the back burner?"

"A fenrir bite is largely physical rather than pith-based and will take more time to heal. I may not be in top form for a while."

I stiffened. "You don't think they'll call the duel before you heal, do you?"

"They'll have their hands full with the fenrir. Let's focus on the emergency at hand."

He had a point. Still, Sertalis wouldn't play fair and would push for anything that gave him an advantage.

Guntram massaged a shoulder. "Speaking of disasters, how is Vincent?"

"Ha ha. You're hilarious. I got him an ambulance. They're taking him to a hospital."

Guntram finally opened his eyes. "Care to explain how he ended up in the path of a fenrir?"

Not really, but I didn't see how I could get out of it. "An uncle had been killed by a wolf. Vincent went to the area to check it out."

"How long ago?"

"I dunno. Recently."

"So they're related?"

"Not by blood." I refused to go into Vincent's whole past with Christy. "Vincent's family is just really close to this guy's, so he's kinda like his uncle."

"But these families have ken, don't they? That's why they stick together."

I sputtered, wondering how he'd reached that accurate conclusion. "I…I don't know…"

Guntram pierced me with his unwavering gaze. "There's no need to be evasive. It's common enough for ken to run in families, and it would certainly explain why a fenrir attacked both this family friend and Vincent himself."

My mind whirled in confusion. "Run in families? But I thought shepherds specifically train teen orphans as eyases."

"We do. Ever heard the phrase, 'Power corrupts?' Humans with ties to the outside world tend to use their Nasci-given abilities for selfish reasons. Thus, we tend to recruit young people with few ties."

"But not me," I pointed out.

Guntram stretched to work out more of his upper body. "There are exceptions, but you know better than most what it means to be different."

I snorted. If I had a dollar for every time someone called me haggard, I could probably buy my own private island. "Okay, but what does this have to do with Vincent's family?"

Guntram leaned forward, a sure sign he was about to give a monologue. "Back in the Onyara Wilds, we didn't recruit families with ken, but we did make alliances with them. Like dryants, they can sometimes sense disturbances in nature before we shepherds could spot it. We called these people 'innates,' and they were like having extra ears and eyes in the forest." Guntram pointed at me. "Vincent comes from an innate family, doesn't he?"

No use hiding it. "But how did you know?"

"I've been having the ravens follow you. I know, for example, that you made quite the scene at a recent family gathering."

Heat rose in my cheeks that had nothing to do with the temperature of the water. "You shouldn't be spying on me. I'm not your eyas anymore."

"But you are under my direct command. You knew I did not approve of your relationship with Vincent."

His tone suggested he believed differently now. "And you've changed your mind?"

"My ravens watched Vincent's family for many hours after you left. They noted minor magic uses, such as one elderly woman stirring lemonade without touching it and another young man lighting a grill with only his fingertip. His relatives are clearly comfortable with pith."

"You're telling me the fenrir attacked both the uncle and Vincent because of their pithways?"

"Correct. What are vaetturs if not magical leeches, feasting on pith-rich animals and dryants? Humans are creatures of Nasci and have pith, of course, but vaetturs largely ignore them because the amount they hold is normally too small to notice, slim pickings. But a human with ken would entice them."

I shivered. "Are you saying Vincent's family smells like a cooking hamburger to a hungry vaettur?"

"Yes, which is why I've been trying to convince the Oracle for years to adopt a position closer to the Onyara Wilds. A relationship between shepherds and innates would benefit both of us. We could protect each other."

"Why hasn't it happened?"

Guntram scowled. "For the same reason many things around here don't change. Tradition. Sertalis hates the idea of mingling with any humans other than full-fledged followers of Nasci."

"But the Oracle makes the decisions. Why doesn't she just force the issue?"

Guntram sighed. "Because she's trying desperately to unite a very divided community in the Talol Wilds. We've lost more shepherds in the decade before you arrived than we can train to replace them. She can't afford petty infighting. The Oracle had already given Tabitha and me generous leeway by allowing us to found the southern homestead. She throws the bone of limited human involvement to Sertalis to keep the peace between the two factions in the long haul."

I groaned. "Ugh. Why is there so much politics? I thought I'd left that all behind with civilized society."

He slouched, lines forming on his face making him appear older. "Where there are people, there are politics."

"So what can we do about Vincent and his family?"

"Your connection to him gives us an opportunity. You can communicate with them in an unofficial capacity. Create a bond that will benefit everyone."

I gave him a sly smile. "Are you asking me to break a rule?"

He huffed into his beard. "Absolutely not. We are not to form any official connections."

"Why don't you do it?"

"Because you are allowed freedom to mingle with normal people given your background. I don't. Also, it would cause a much bigger stir for an augur of the southern homestead to forge such a connection. But an upstart shepherd has a lot more wiggle room."

I sank down to my chin in the water. "Great. I'm already a troublemaker, so what's one more mark against me, right?"

"I would not make you do anything you don't want to do."

Which, of course, was the whole point. I was already in deep with Vincent anyway. Keeping an eye on him and his family didn't really change my behavior much.

Plus, it had one other added benefit. "Guess you won't mind me hanging out with Vincent so much, huh?"

He frowned at me, trying to gauge how much to let me get away with. "As long as you keep it a largely professional relationship."

I thought of Fechin catching Vincent and me kissing before. "If you're having ravens following me, you already know that boat has sailed."

"It would be best if you were objective. Because innates aren't trained like shepherds or forgers, their pithways develop slightly differently than ours. Every once in a while, they can even develop strange abilities that we don't have sigils for."

I rubbed water on my face to hide what I'm sure was an expression that would give me away. Did Guntram know Vincent could freeze vaetturs, like the fenrir attacking the pickup? "And what should I do if I see anything like that?"

"Be wary. It indicates you are dealing with a potentially powerful human with untapped magical abilities. Don't give them any reason to use those powers for selfish reasons, or they might become a problem we must deal with."

The way he said 'deal with' made it very clear the answer would be a permanent solution. Awesome.

I got my grimace under control so I could face Guntram again. "Don't worry. I'll be careful."

Guntram did not appear convinced. "You would not be my first choice for this task. You already have too many impulsive tendencies. And you really should rethink your emotions regarding Vincent Garcia."

"Sure, I'll get right on that," I said, standing up with my back turned to him. "But shouldn't someone go back to Sipho's and give everyone an update?"

Guntram nodded. "Yes." He groaned as he got back to his feet.

"You don't have to go, Guntram. You can stay here

and heal."

"This is my duty," he insisted. "We'll need to form even tighter security around the lesions until this is all over. We'll both go."

CHAPTER 16

GUNTRAM KEPT PACE with me through the wisp channels back to the southern homestead, but I could tell he was in pain. He nursed a limp when he thought I wasn't looking, and he drew extra air sigils to mask the sound of his ragged breathing. I tried to slow down, but he yelled at me to quit dawdling. Guntram wouldn't let something as minor as a wolf bite slow him down.

His kidama picked up on it too, swarming close and flinging feathers into my vision. Normally I would have shooed them away, but I understood exactly how they felt.

I worried about Guntram too.

Fortunately, shepherds had created a very straightforward path that only required a little over an hour hike between the two homesteads. It made sense to cut down on travel time, given that we technically worked together sometimes.

I wondered why it wasn't even shorter though. "Why doesn't someone create a direct wisp channel between the northern homestead and the southern one?"

"Wisp channel creation is not a simple task. It takes an incredible amount of energy to create one, for starters, and then they must be maintained with upkeep sigils."

"You mean like we do with defensive sigils?" One of my least favorite chores is to run around the wilderness drawing circles. These temporary sigils made it hard for vaetturs to create breaches into our world but were a huge pain to maintain. Because of our lesion issues, we'd had to put defensive sigil drawing on hold. I shuddered imagining the sheer volume of work required to bring them all back to Guntram's satisfaction when this was over.

"Yes, like defensive sigils. Although wisp channels don't require quite as frequent reinforcements, it is still quite the task for the augurs and Oracles. And the farther the distance between them, the more often and more pith you must expend to keep them open."

That explained why most wisp channels stretched 20-30 miles at most. "So hypothetically, if you created a wisp channel that connected Mt. Rainier to the Willamette Valley, what would that take?"

"Near constant upkeep and charms' worth of pith. And be thankful that is so. What if the northern homestead could visit Sipho's whenever they pleased?"

"Good point. Let's never speak of this again, okay?"

We honestly didn't do much more speaking than that. We arrived at the homestead in the late afternoon, and Guntram immediately went for a quick soak in the hot spring. He said it was "to think," but we both knew the relatively short trip had winded him. Tired, but not enough for another dip, I left Guntram to his private soak and instead searched for a spot to make a phone call.

It never ceased to amaze me how sporadic phone reception can be out in the woods. I've had days where I get four bars inside the homestead and others where I had to hike miles outside the boundaries for a bit of service. When I finally found a signal in the middle of the apple orchard, I placed a few calls to check up on Vincent. I found the hospital he was taken to and learned he was listed in stable condition.

After I hung up, I realized his family should know what

had happened to him. Although I wasn't a huge fan of his mother, they deserved to know. I dialed Oscar's work number, the only contact I had for the rest of the Garcia clan.

Vincent's cousin answered with his cheery professional voice. "Hello, Soto Plumbing. How can I help you?"

"Oscar, it's Ina." There was no way to break this gently, but you had to give me points for trying. "You know how Vincent went looking for the wolf that killed Thomas?"

Silence hung on the other end.

"Oscar?" I asked. "You still there?"

"I, uh," he stammered. "I don't know what you're talking about."

I rubbed my temple with my free hand. "Oscar, this isn't time to be scared of The Man. Vincent told me all about Uncle Thomas's illegal living situation and how you all sent him to investigate his death."

"Oh," Oscar said lamely.

"And it gets worse." I took a deep breath, deciding to keep things simple for now. "Vincent found the wolf in the worst way. It attacked him."

"What?" Oscar's cry of surprise forced me to move the phone away from my ear. He continued with a string of one-word exclamations. "How? When? Where?"

"He's doing fine, but he's at a hospital in Washington." I rushed to provide the name and details before Oscar shattered my eardrums.

When I finished, Oscar was talking more to himself than me. "I gotta call his mom. And his grandma. Everyone's gonna be so upset."

I got another word in edgewise, trying to extract myself. "I just called to let you know. Catch ya later, okay?"

"Ina, wait!" Oscar yelled before I could hang up. I made the poor choice of staying on the line. "How did you know about any of this? Did you go up with him or something? Are you guys that serious?"

I'm surprised my blush didn't catch the phone on fire. "It's not exactly like that—" I tried to explain.

But Oscar had moved onto his next train of thought. "Thanks for letting me know. I'll inform the others."

Then he hung up.

Well, that didn't go as planned, but I guess it could have been worse. Conjecture on our relationship aside, Vincent's family would keep tabs on him in the hospital. He wouldn't wake up alone. I could live with that.

My good Samaritan deed done for the day, I decided to check up on Sipho and Callum. They needed to know about the fenrir.

The minute I stepped into the forge, I could taste the excitement. The two forgers were bent over the far table, sputtering excitedly to each other. They'd created an anthill-sized mound of dirt in front of them, presumably from the lesions, and waved their hands over it as if warming by a fire. Callum even squealed in delight at one point. Both mountain lions, instead of lazing about, wound around their legs and rubbed their faces into bare legs as if to absorb some of that positive energy.

No one, not even the cats, noticed me enter, so I knocked on the door frame. "Did I come at a bad time?"

The cougars yowled at being surprised. Sipho and Callum nearly knocked heads as they whipped around, but even that didn't diminish the goofy grins on their faces.

Sipho blinked at me, eyes twice as large from behind magnifying eyeglasses. "We've had a breakthrough, and it's thanks to you, Ina!"

Finally, people happy to see me. I caught their infectious cheer. "I don't know why I'm smiling, but yay!"

Callum grabbed a bundle of gray plastic and waved its folded edges at me. "It's like I told you. The fire blanket held the key. We're close to crafting a damp ward that will seal the lesions for good."

"Let me demonstrate." Sipho motioned me toward the

work bench. "Callum and I have been trying to sense Nasci's lifeblood from this sample taken from the lesion near Mohawk. Can you feel anything?"

I raised my hand over the dirt. "Nothing but that's not unusual. I don't normally feel much coming out of the lesion."

"But we forgers do," Callum said. He also hovered a palm above the mound. "I don't feel anything."

Sipho nodded. "It's as if this is normal dirt." She then dug her fingertips into the soil to withdraw a thumbnail-sized square. As she shook specks of soil off it, I recognized it as a tightly folded bit of fire blanket held into shape by thin wire, almost like a teeny Christmas present for a steampunk mouse.

"The fire blanket stopped the bad mojo you feel around lesions?" I asked. "How is that possible?"

"The fiberglass outer shell keeps Nasci's energy in the tungsten."

"What tungsten? You mean the wire?"

Sipho took a pair of tweezers and eased the strands apart to expose a small metal slab like the charms that hung around my neck. When she dipped the bare metal into the dirt, super faint etchings lit up like LED lights.

"That's the tungsten."

I leaned in close and squinted at it. "Whoa! Those etchings are so microscopic."

"Microwhat?" Sipho asked.

"Never mind." I waved away the word. The last thing I wanted was to explain what a microscope was and have to buy one for Sipho with Mom's credit card.

Sipho pointed back to the bright charm. "Without the fire blanket, some of the energy escapes. Any energy that does can still be absorbed by the surrounding environment, and the lesion will fester. When I figure out how to scale this ward up to absorb an entire lesion, we will finally have a solution that should seal it for good."

"Isn't it amazing?" Callum exclaimed, beaming with

pride. In his excitement, his shoulder accidentally brushed up against mine. He jerked away as if I'd punched him.

"Something wrong?" I asked as I shifted back to give him more room.

Ignoring me, Callum addressed Sipho. "Touch Ina's hoodie. You feel that?"

Sipho gently brushed her hand against my elbow and then recoiled. "Yes. She's steeped in it."

"Steeped in what?" I asked.

Callum bounced on his heels excitedly. "Give her the ward!"

Sipho brightened. "Of course." She folded the fire blanket and wire back over the metal. Then she shoved the ward into my hand.

It felt like…holding something light. Nothing more, nothing less. I might as well have been holding a piece of scrap paper. "Should I be experiencing something?"

Well, I did in a way. Sipho and Callum patted my arms as if I were some exotic pet. Weirded out though I was, I didn't start pushing them away until their gentle touches became grabby.

"It even works on Ina!" Callum exclaimed.

"Yes. Completely subdued," Sipho said. She reached for the ward.

"Hey!" I skipped out of reach, the prototype still in my hand. "Mind telling me what's going on?"

Callum pointed to my muddy hoodie. "When's the last time you washed that thing?"

"I've been busy!" Despite my protests, it took some genuine effort not to sniff my collar to check and make sure I didn't reek of body odor. "Why do you care?"

"Your clothes exude Nasci's lifeblood because you've been guarding the lesion with it for so long," Sipho said. "We just confirmed giving you the damp ward stops its presence on you too, like the dirt."

I glanced down at my attire. "Now that you mention it, Elif said she could sense it on me."

Sipho stiffened at the mention of the northern forger. "You saw Elif?"

It dawned on me that I hadn't told them the bad news. I handed Sipho the damp ward back. "I hate to burst your happy bubble, but we've got another problem. The northern homestead's dealing with a fenrir right now."

Sipho gasped, the whites of her eyes huge. "Where?"

"Around Colville National Forest."

"Is it heading south?"

"I honestly don't know. So far, the north seems to think they have it handled. Guntram and I just came back to tell you as a precaution."

"We'll need more than precautions where a fenrir is concerned." Sipho fiddled with the ward in her hand and bit her lip.

Callum looked at her, and then at me with a confused frown. "What's going on?"

"A fenrir's one of the baddest vaetturs around," I explained. "Super fast and able to open new breaches back to Letum at will. It tends to leave shepherd bodies behind."

"And I don't like it this close to the lesions," Sipho added. "I don't care how confident the north is. This could spell disaster for the entire Talol Wilds. Callum, you will cease all homestead maintenance immediately and help me replicate two more of these wards."

"But this is only a prototype. It isn't strong enough to block out all the energy from the lesions. We need time to perfect it."

"Time that's now run out," Sipho said. "We must mask as much of Nasci's lifeblood as we can immediately so that the fenrir doesn't find it."

"We don't want another chumal situation on our hands," I whispered.

Sipho's expression darkened. "If the fenrir absorbs Nasci's lifeblood, it will make those vaetturs look like the insects they were. Callum and I will work through the night if we have to, but we'll get these new damp wards distributed to the three sites as soon as possible. And then we'll devote ourselves to the final upgraded designs. We can't take chances, not with a fenrir on the loose."

CHAPTER 17

GUNTRAM WAS REWORKING the lesion guard duty schedule when I ran into him an hour later. He wanted to put two shepherds on each lesion but couldn't figure out a way to do it with our limited numbers. Guntram grumbled but made do with the next best thing: expanded deployment of kidama. He'd already sent more of his ravens out as scouts around each lesion, giving them explicit instructions to be on the lookout for the fenrir. He told me he'd send word to Azar to do the same with her newts.

I witnessed the animals in action when I guarded the Noti lesion that evening. Even in the waning evening light, I spied plenty of rough-skinned newts, their orange bellies bright as they crawled through the fallen autumn leaves. Ravens also cawed overhead in large quantities, many settling into the treetops as the night wore on. I dreaded the racket they'd make at dawn, but I supposed it was better than getting surprise attacked by a fenrir.

I sent several texts to Vincent before I nodded off but wasn't really surprised when he didn't answer. He'd had a rough day after all. But as the sun rose and the pesky ravens squawked for a new day, I couldn't stop worrying about him. I sent more texts, and around nine o'clock, I even tried calling him outright, but his phone went straight to voicemail. I called the hospital about him, but besides listing his condition as still stable, they wouldn't reveal much else.

That's why when Euchloe came to relieve me a few hours later, I wasted my break to check on Vincent in person. I needed to see with my own eyes that he'd recovered from the fenrir attack.

Traveling there was a pain since he was located smack down in the middle of Colville, Washington. While not much larger than Kettle Falls, the town was spread out on a heavily developed wide plain in between the surrounding mountains. The nearest wisp channel only took me to the edge of town, and with no public transportation, I had to walk the rest of the way. The hour hike took me past a sprawling golf course (because there's some law that all rural towns in the Pacific Northwest require a golf course). Then I trekked up and down the hills of a quiet neighborhood before finally reaching the hospital. By the time I got there, I had to draw a breeze to cool myself off despite it being a brisk day.

The small regional hospital looked more like a high school than a sleek mecca of modern medicine. With its blocky structure, 70s glass paneled windows, and red brick façade, it clearly needed an upgrade. Cranky and tired, I lugged myself through the quiet automatic doors.

Despite being a bit dated on the outside, the inside had obviously been remodeled. The sleek floors and walls had all been done in shades of forgettable tan and were impeccably clean. I approached a row of empty floral-patterned chairs leading to the reception desk.

The middle-aged receptionist with the headset strapped to her ear gave me a deer-in-the-headlights look. "Can I help you?" she asked, clearly hoping she couldn't help at all.

I didn't have the emotional bandwidth to wonder at her

behavior. "I'm here to see Vincent Garcia."

The corner of her lips twitched. "Of course, you are."

Her resigned tone caught me off guard. "Huh?"

She gestured toward my ripped shorts and hoodie. "Would you prefer going home for a change before seeing him? Visiting hours won't end for a while."

Seriously, what was with everyone criticizing my appearance? I'd even changed into this spare hoodie, and it had only half the dirt smears as the one from yesterday.

"Lady, it's been a long day. Just give me his room number."

Since I look about sixteen years old to a lot of folks, I didn't actually expect my frustrated request to work. So, I was surprised when she raised a hand immediately in defeat. "No offense. It was only a suggestion." Then she gave me curt directions to Vincent's room and told me I could find complimentary breakfast items in the visitor's lounge.

Something besides her attitude made the whole encounter seem strange. As I navigated the maze of hallways and stairwells, I realized she knew Vincent's room number without even typing on her computer. Unless that headset plugged her brain directly into a database somewhere, that shouldn't be possible.

I entered a different wing of the hospital, passing the lounge the receptionist had mentioned. A gaggle of people chatted inside, but they'd closed the door so only vague blobs moved behind distorted glass. Much as I would have enjoyed bad coffee and stale donuts (I'm always desperate for food), I didn't feel like socializing. I headed straight into Vincent's room.

Vincent and I shared way too many hospital memories. The first time I'd visited him in one, he'd looked like a superhero recovering after the climax of a movie, dramatically slumped forward in sleep. Not this time. He dozed behind guard rails that seemed like prison bars, dark circles under his eyes. His breathing came in spurts of wheezes. Machines beeped in an irritating rhythm around him, flashing ominous vital statistics.

My own blood pumped louder in my ears than the machines as I crept up to his bedside. I laid gentle hand over his. At least his skin felt warm underneath mine. My touch didn't disturb him at first, but after a few minutes he shifted his legs underneath the thin blanket. His fingers reflexively wound against mine.

"Ina?" he whispered through cracked lips.

I smiled as brightly as I could. "Hey."

I leaned over, and he rubbed a hand over my cheek. It sent ripples of pleasure down my pithways. The weight of recent events lifted from my shoulders, giving me a brief moment of peace.

Then it disappeared as panic settled over Vincent. He pushed himself up with his free hand so we were about the same height. "Why are you here?" he asked, a hint of accusation in his voice.

"I was worried about you. You weren't answering your phone."

He blinked, glancing at the side tables around him. "I don't even know where my phone is. Maybe someone in my…" he trailed off. "It might be better if you left. Now."

I let go of his hand. "I hiked all the way here into the middle of nowhere Washington, and all you have to say is 'See you later?'"

He pushed back his greasy jet-black hair. "I'm happy that you care. Honestly. It's just that I don't want to cause a scene."

Realization dawned. "Is that your family in the lounge? Don't worry about it. I'm the one that called them here. I'll behave, I promise."

"You're not the one I'm worried about."

I opened my mouth to reply when a familiar voice of disapproval cut into our conversation. "So, you decided to show up."

A short Hispanic woman straddling middle-age and

senior citizenship glared at us from the doorway. Her white-streaked hair betrayed that time would eventually win. She had the opposite of laugh lines on her face, a permanent frown underscoring her general personality. Today there was extra malice in that expression.

"Mom," Vincent called from his bed. "Be nice."

Her frown relaxed into worry marks above her eyebrows. "How are you doing, baby?"

"Better after a nap," he said as his mom approached. I took a step back as she forced her way to where I'd been standing.

She petted his hair. "The doctor said if you do good today, we can take you home."

Vincent grimaced. "You're not badgering the hospital staff again, are you?"

"Of course not. How could you suggest such a thing?"

He gave her a good, long look. "Because the night nurse told me how you demanded to take me home against orders last night."

She waved her hand dismissively. "They don't understand that family knows what's best."

"The doctors know what's best. Please listen to them, Mom."

Despite my irritation, I felt a pang of sympathy for Vincent. I thought I had an overbearing mom, but Teresa Garcia might chew mine up and spit her out.

And then Vincent further surprised me. "And you need to give Ina a break. Like I said last night, she's the one who saved me from the wolf. You should be thanking her."

"That's the drugs talking, baby."

"It's not the drugs." Vincent shooed her away and motioned me forward. For a second, I didn't think Teresa would relent. Outrage flashed in her rigid stance, but she reluctantly stepped aside.

I had no desire to step into this mess. "Maybe I should go…"

"Absolutely not," Vincent said, his voice the most firm

it had been since I stepped into the room. He reached out a longing hand toward me.

I couldn't resist. I tiptoed back to his bedside, and he grabbed my hand.

Vincent faced his mother off as squarely as he could in a hospital bed. "Ina saved my life. I owe her for that. And even more important, I care about her."

"Vincente—" his mother chided.

He cut her off. "She's my girlfriend."

Honestly, all three of us were stunned by the declaration. Me because I hadn't officially known we were back together again. His mother because she looked as if Vincent had slapped her. And Vincent because he suddenly appeared very remorseful.

"That is," he added, gazing up at me, "if she'll still have me after how I treated her."

Tears stung, but I refused to let them fall. I squeezed his hand instead. I wanted to tell him I cared about him too, but all that came out was, "Sure."

Vincent squeezed back.

In the tense standoff that followed, none of us noticed the uptick in machine whirring and beeping. A passing nurse, however, must have heard something because she poked her head in. "Something the matter in here?"

Teresa pointed at me. "She's disturbing my son."

"Mom!" Vincent protested. "Did you not hear a word I said?"

The nurse stepped into the room to check Vincent's chart. "It might be best if we all give Mr. Garcia a little space."

I sighed, turning to Vincent. "Sorry about this."

"Don't be. This is my fault." He gave one final tug before letting me go. The monitor indicated his heart rate increased as he did so.

The nurse frowned at me as the machine protested the change. "Everybody out."

Teresa kept complaining, but we both made for the

exit. "I'll call you, Ina!" Vincent yelled after me, causing his mother to fume.

The nurse insisted on escorting us back to the common lounge, where I was not surprised to see the door wide open and a flock of Vincent's relatives inside. Unfortunately, Oscar's friendly face was not among them. They stared at me in shock as Teresa let out a string of Spanish that I'm sure contained swear words.

"I'm sorry," I said to the nurse as she walked away.

She paused to give me her best authoritative stance. "If you're really sorry, you will give him some space to heal." Then she wandered off back toward his room.

That seemed like my cue to escape. I walked briskly away from the lounge doorway and back out of the wing.

"Hey!" Teresa's sharp cry rang out as I rounded a corner. I picked up my pace, hoping she wouldn't come after me, but sharp heels clicking on the vinyl floor indicated otherwise. "You! The dog that invaded our family!"

Only she didn't say dog exactly. I don't know much Spanish, but I knew that word. I stopped next to a large potted plant, my muscles tense as I waited for her to reach conversational distance.

"Good thing I like dogs," I said in as flat a tone as I could muster. "Otherwise, I might get upset."

She ignored my sarcasm. "Don't you believe for a second that I don't see what's going on around here."

"I thought Vincent made it pretty clear. We're dating."

"You're manipulating him!" I could have imagined it, but I swear I felt a slight rumble in the floor beneath me as Teresa aimed her painted fingernail at me. "That's the only reason he's in the hospital."

"He's hurt because you sent him to find a freaking wolf. Alone, I might add."

"He's a big boy. He could have handled it."

"The strongest people I know couldn't just 'handle' that wolf alone," I said before realizing I shouldn't just be spilling shepherd secrets. I shook my head to clear my thoughts. "Look, what's important is that I care about Vincent."

"Keep telling yourself that," Teresa sneered. "The ones who really love Vincent know that he should be with Christy."

"Are you referring to the dog who cheated on him?" Only I used her little Spanish word. Two could play at that game.

Teresa's face turned a vibrant shade of red. This time, there was no mistaking the tremors underfoot. Earth pith washed off her tan skin as clearly as if I'd thrust my hands into soil.

She directed all that energy on me with a clawed hand. "Take that back."

I shouldn't have goaded her. I should have backed off. Instead, I leaned toward her. "Make me."

It was surreal, watching a woman in church clothes lift a clod of dirt from the potted plant. She flung it toward me without so much as a sigil. Just like Guntram had said, magic ran heavy in this family.

As impressive as that power was, though, I'd faced off against Darby, an earth shepherd prodigy, and survived. I drew a countersigil, negating both the mini-tremors and forcing the wad of dirt back to the plant rather than into my face as Teresa intended.

It took her a few seconds to realize I'd countered her attack. Her triumphant expression twisted into one of disbelief. She tried to lift the dirt again, but I swatted it back down.

A corner of my lips upturned in a humorless smile. "Your family's not the only one with powers."

Teresa stepped back as if I'd sprouted horns and a forked tail. Her voice dropped to the hushed tones of disbelief, whispering what might have been prayers in Spanish.

I rolled my eyes. "Oh, come on. Don't tell me you're

freaking out because I've got more mojo than you."

She made the sign of the cross. "Leave my family alone."

The slight whimper in her tone undid me. I can deal with angry people, no problem, but not someone's abject terror. I slowly backed away.

"I'm not going to hurt Vincent," I tried to reassure her, but she was already fleeing down the corridor.

As I left the hospital, I tried to reconcile what had happened. I'd come to check on Vincent, and not only found out he wasn't doing so well, but now his mom thought I was some sort of monster.

"Sorry, Guntram," I muttered. "I am the world's worst diplomat."

CHAPTER 18

I DECIDED TO stress eat before returning to Sipho's. It was several hours before my next shift, and I'd earned it. I wandered down Colville's Main Street (the other requirement for all rural towns) and couldn't find any fast food chains, but at least there was a decent selection of local joints. I settled on a Mexican restaurant with a cheery pseudo-Southwestern façade and ordered their enchilada lunch special. I had my pick of the booths and chose to sit under a terra cotta sun. I ate more than a healthy serving of chips and salsa before the main dish arrived and polished that off, too.

I appreciated all the work Sipho and Callum do planting food on the homestead, really I did, but nothing beats situational depression better than an American-sized meal.

Afterwards, I strolled the sidewalks toward the wisp channel, taking my time to digest. At least Vincent and I were okay. I wondered if I should have given him more flack for acting so emo at the beach but getting clobbered by a fenrir seemed like an oversized way to pay for it. I was just happy he'd survived the experience.

Still, I was supposed to make inroads with Vincent's

entire family. I didn't think I'd ever get Teresa on board, but maybe I could establish better relationships with people like Oscar. If vaetturs could go after Vincent's family, then Guntram was right: the more we watched each other's backs, the better off we all would be. Uncle Thomas's death proved that.

After retreating back into the woods, a chill autumn breeze penetrated my hoodie. I drew an inner heat sigil, the fire pith creating a sensation like drinking hot coffee. My route took me back over the Columbia Gorge. I paused on a bluff to watch the mighty river snake through the mountains. East of my position, Mt. Hood rose like a god among hills, her snow-capped peak a testament to her size. It's a view few would witness but was part of my everyday life.

Despite it all, being a shepherd really did have its perks.

Something scurried through the brush. A slender brown doe stepped out into the light. She had bat-like ears with faint green glitter marks protruding from each side of her slender face. Those sparkles dotted down her flanks, ending in a white sunburst pattern on her rump. If that wasn't enough of a giveaway that she was a dryant, her bright glowing eyes would have done the trick.

"Piyax," I bowed my head in respect to the white-tailed deer dryant. It made sense I'd run into her in Tabitha's old stomping grounds, the region that would transfer with Darby to the northern homestead. The last time I'd seen Piyax, she'd been giving Darby her Shepherd Trial. That showed how deep their connection was.

The dryant marched toward me. She did not seem frightened, but I could sense something else in her swagger. Worry, maybe? She bumped her nose into my shoulder, then gave me a few licks with her rough tongue.

I steadied myself by patting her side. "Whoa, there," I whispered, wishing I could speak directly to her the way augurs did with their kidama. "Is something wrong?"

She arched her thick neck toward Mt. Hood, ears

flicking in agitation. She grunted, glanced back at me, and then focused back in on the snowy peak.

"A vaettur on Mt. Hood?" I asked.

She continued to stare blankly.

"Something else then?"

She squeaked an affirmation. Then, without another word, she trotted off. Not the pace of an animal frightened, but more like she'd delivered her message and had no more to say.

"Glad we had this talk," I called after her.

Of course, I had no idea what any of that was about. I wondered if I should take a detour up the mountain to check things out.

But then I stopped myself. And do what? Mt. Hood covered a stupid large area. I'd be lucky to cover a handful of square miles before my next lesion shift. Better to just tell Guntram or Azar about Piyax's strange behavior when I saw them.

But by the time I arrived at Sipho's under the midday sun, I'd forgotten about the whole incident. Instead, I focused on the crude wooden "Out to Forage" sign in front of the forge, indicating Sipho and Callum had gone to implement the wards they'd been working on. Nur rubbed against my legs but left once I entered the lodge.

I found a note on the counter telling me the shift schedule had changed, and I had one at Whittaker Creek in a half hour. So much for a nap. After downing a cup of tea and some jam toast, I trudged my way westward. Once at the lesion, I relieved a grumpy Zibel from his post. He mumbled something about food as he shuffled off.

I hunkered down against a tree, hoping I could still sleep, but my body decided to betray me by remaining wide awake.

Fine, body. If that's the way you want to play, you'll have to make yourself useful.

And that's why, tired as I was, I devoted myself to some sigil practice. It takes an incredible amount of time to master new sigils, and I had to learn via practice like any other shepherd. I'd been trying to master insular strokes, a kind of cursive sigil writing, so I could learn how to form mist like my buddy Wuaro of the Bitai Wilds. He'd shown me that writing simple Vs could create a light drizzle from my hand if I wrote them correctly, but so far all I'd been able to do was get my palms wet. I kept at it for at least half an hour, growing more frustrated as I failed time and again.

I wiped my wet palm against my shorts in disgust. "Who wanted to master that sigil anyway?"

"Spoken like a true haggard."

I scowled as I recognized that airy voice. "You sure love popping up out of nowhere like a gremlin, don't you, Elif?"

Her dark robes emerged from the forest gloom, accentuating her bony extremities. "You seemed so lonely talking to yourself, I thought you might enjoy an actual reply for a change."

I stifled a snort. That was a decent burn for such an uptight twig. "You're kinda far from your little fiefdom, aren't you? These are southern homestead lands."

Elif sniffed, almost appearing to float with her legs hidden underneath her long skirt. "We northerners have every right to be here, just as you wander onto our lands."

I mock bowed. "What brings you to our neck of the woods, Esteemed One?"

She produced a small clay jar and an abnormally large spoon from within her draping sleeves. "I require a sample of the lesion dirt."

Something about the way she said it, as if she expected me to argue with her, produced the intended results. "Why?"

"It is none of your concern."

I stepped into her path, coming in between her and the bare patch of earth where new plants refused to grow. I glared defiantly up her nose. "Try me."

She moved a step to the left. I followed. She tried right. Ditto.

Growling, she said, "You're obstructing our ability to catch the fenrir."

I lifted an eyebrow. "What does lesion dirt have to do with catching it?"

Her voice took on an air of superiority. "The fenrir continues to elude us, so Sertalis and I have devised a clever plan to lure the wretched vaettur out into the open."

Was she saying what I thought she was saying? "You're going to bait the fenrir using lesion dirt?"

She used my momentary distraction to skirt past me. "It is a solid strategy. I could detect lesion energy on you at a great distance the other day. The fenrir will be even more sensitive. If I create a ward to amplify the essence of Nasci's lifeblood, it will surely show itself. All we need is an open area so it cannot escape. Then we can banish it for good."

"Wait, you want to augment the lesion's scent? Isn't that the opposite of what a ward should do?"

"There are damp wards and there are amp wards. Do not strain yourself figuring out which kind I am creating."

As she bent over to collect soil, the only way I could stop her from taking the lesion dirt was to attack her. It was tempting, oh so tempting, but no. Guntram would kill me.

Instead, fists formed at my sides as she scooped dirt into the jar. "If you fail, you could lead the fenrir right to the real lesions."

Elif smirked. "We will not fail." She strode back toward the darkness from which she emerged.

"And how can you guarantee that?"

She threw me a smile full of teeth. "Because we are northern shepherds. We know what we are doing."

And then she was gone.

I trusted Elif's confidence about as far as I could toss her. It wasn't a completely flippant statement. I could probably chuck her a decent distance with an air sigil. But then again, she might have something to counteract me and weigh her down. She might be annoying, but she had real forger chops.

I had to tell Guntram about her plan. Problem was, I had just started my shift. Abandoning the post was highly irresponsible, especially given the north's half-baked scheme.

A flurry of feathers above me in a hemlock reminded me I wouldn't leave the area without sentries. Guntram's ravens and Azar's newt counterparts scurried around the peripheries of my vision, alerting me to their presence.

I leaped to my feet. "I gotta rush back to the homestead. Can you guys hold this area for twenty minutes?"

A large black bird broke off from his friends to land on a whipplevine and squawk at me. Fechin, Guntram's leading henchbird. Of course, he'd assign this bird to watch me.

"I gotta warn Guntram about Elif's plan."

Fechin hopped around and screeched away, clearly not happy.

"Well if I don't warn them, who will?"

Fechin gave me his bird stink eye. Then he lurched upward into the air, making a big show of heading in the direction of the homestead.

Oh yeah, I realized sheepishly. Fechin could telepathically communicate with Guntram. It made a lot more sense for him to tell Guntram than me running off.

Sufficiently cowed by the raven, I settled back down to whittle the rest of my shift away watching a patch of dirt. Trust me, it was as exciting as it sounded. Fechin returned a few hours later, cawing at me to indicate he'd done his job.

That was about all I could do regarding Elif. Much as I wanted to, I couldn't babysit the northern homestead by myself.

Baot relieved me in the early twilight hours, obnoxiously cheery as usual. I wished I could borrow his upbeat personality for times like these as I hauled it back to the homestead. Again, I found the place devoid of shepherds, although I saw a light flickering in the forge window. I thought about saying hello to the forgers but opted for the hot spring instead. Then, after a quick pat on Kam's head as she prowled the grounds, I went to sleep, banking that someone would wake me for my next shift.

CHAPTER 19

A TEETH-RATTLING banging on the bedroom door jolted me out of a very deep sleep. "Ina, get up! We are needed!"

I flailed so hard, I fell out of bed. The blanket became entangled around my torso, and in my panicked, partially alert state, I struggled to get it off.

The rapping repeated itself. "There's no time for goofing around! Let's go!"

Finally managing to free myself, I crawled in the early morning light toward the door. Using the handle as leverage to stand, I pushed it open to find Guntram glaring down through his beard, an unconscious wind ruffling his tattered cloak.

"It's dumb o'clock. You know I don't function well at this hour. Why throw me on guard duty now?"

But I was talking to his back as he stalked down the hallway. "We're not going to the lesions."

Both my brain and my body scrambled after him. "What?"

"The northern shepherds plan to draw the fenrir out soon."

Logic slowly seeped into my sleep-deprived brain cells.

"Right. You got my message from Fechin. But what's the rush?"

"I traveled to their homestead yesterday and tried to stop them, but Sertalis has everyone convinced his plan is sound. He's taking almost everyone from the north there to draw out the fenrir with the amp ward as we speak."

I crammed on my boots and strode behind him across the homestead meadows. Dew dampened the top of my socks as the higher grasses brushed against them.

"And the Oracle's just letting him do this?" I asked.

"She's going to create a barrier once the fenrir enters the trap. They all believe this will prevent the vaettur from leaving the area."

I snorted. "They really think a simple firewall will contain the fenrir?"

Guntram gave me the I-taught-you-better glare. "This is the Oracle we're talking about. She can conjure not only a fire barrier, but one of water, wind, and earth all combined. Once in place, not even Sertalis and I can get through it, it's so pith-heavy with all four elements. She can also make it span for miles, although not for very long before it taxes her completely."

"Oh." The thought of an elemental shield that not even an augur could pass through did sound pretty legit. "Actually, that sounds pretty solid. Maybe their kooky plan will work."

His scowl deepened, clearly disappointed in my intelligence. "They're going to lure the fenrir to Mt. Hood."

I snapped to attention. "That's where Piyax was fixated on yesterday."

Guntram stopped in his tracks, clearly not expecting this non sequitur. "Excuse me?"

I told him about my run in with the deer dryant. "She clearly wanted to send a message about Mt. Hood, but I didn't understand it, so I forgot about it."

"It's likely a warning." Guntram resumed his pace and

then some.

We left the homestead boundaries, diving under whispering trees as Guntram's breeze stirred the leaves left on their branches. I wondered at my mentor's increasingly agitated state. "Are you really that worried about their plan? I mean, if the Oracle is with them, it can't be all bad."

"The northern shepherds forget how powerful a vaettur will become if they get access to Nasci's lifeblood," Guntram said.

"But Mt. Hood doesn't have a lesion."

"Not yet. But think, Ina. What do all the lesion locations have in common?"

"They're all places that Rafe ripped open the earth to access magma."

"And where was the first place he tried to do that?"

I paled, remembering the awful tragedy that took Tabitha's life. "Mt. Hood. So why would the northern shepherds try to lure the fenrir there?"

"Because the fenrir was spotted recently in the Columbia Gorge, and it's the highest open ground to draw it out. Elif's amp ward will send a signal down all sides of the mountain, draping the entire region with the lesion's scent."

"They don't see the location as a problem?"

Guntram pointed us toward a bobbing set of twinkling blue lights in the distance. "They believe they'll be fine since there is no lesion right now. They don't know from experience how quickly one can crop up."

It's true. We'd gone from zero open lesions to three in a matter of weeks. Sipho had sworn she'd sealed them all and was dismayed they could all reopen on their own.

Guntram made a beeline for the wisp channel. "Even if we are wrong about their plan, it will not hurt to have a few extra shepherds on hand. We must hope for the best but brace for the worst."

We had to pause our conversation as we both jumped

through the lights, reappearing underneath a grove of poplar trees a few dozen miles north and next to a valley stream.

"But why me?" I asked. "If you're expecting trouble, why not bring Azar with you?"

"We need solid coverage at each of our three lesions. I have Azar at one, Baot at another, and both Euchloe and Zibel stationed at the third."

"Still, you'd think it would be smarter strategy to bring the two heaviest hitters from the south if you're expecting trouble on Mt. Hood."

"That's one strategy. The other is to rouse the known agitators into actions."

Sometimes, Guntram's flair for the dramatic was too much. "Agitators?"

"You and I are already under intense scrutiny from the north. Our presence will be regarded as part and parcel to our personalities. Azar, however, is considered a more logical and calm shepherd. As our newest augur, it is to our advantage that she maintain that reputation."

"And what about my reputation?"

The side of Guntram's lip upturned into a sly smile. "We're playing right into yours."

I glared at him. "First the innates, and now this. You're getting really good at throwing me under the bus."

"I don't know what public transport has to do with this, but you are a rebel, Ina. You've built your entire magical abilities upon that foundation. Generally, we work around that disadvantage, but every once in a while, I get to leverage it as a pro instead of a con."

I sighed. Much as I hated to admit it, he had a point. "You don't have to look so gleeful about it."

When Guntram chuckled, it morphed into a bit of a cough. He stumbled, and it took a second for him to straighten out. When he did, I noticed him limp.

I couldn't hide the worry in my voice. "Are you sure you're up to this? You got snacked on by a fenrir not long ago."

"I'm fine," Guntram insisted, all mirth gone from his expression. I understood that as an end to the conversation, so I took it as such. But I didn't like it. Not when we were going to a place where a fenrir might gain access to Nasci's lifeblood.

CHAPTER 20

EMBARKING FROM THE last wisp channel that took us to Mt. Hood, I could just feel something was wrong. It wasn't concrete like one of the five senses, but an oppressive weight, the physical manifestation of dread and foreboding. It was like watching a graphic horror movie late at night.

Only this washed over me on the bright and sunny slopes of Oregon's largest mountain. We'd made it up past the tree line, the landscape full of volcanic rocks and scratchy shrubs that blended into the snowpack above. Sure, it was chilly, but it shouldn't have felt "haunted house" cold.

Guntram must have sensed it too because he drew his tattered cloak around him tighter. "It's begun. Elif has set off the amplification ward."

My mentor blew himself up the 65-degree rock face with an air blast. I drew earth sigils to scramble up the wall instead, still not great at my flying dismount. I'd barely flung my upper body over the ridge when Guntram landed next to me and helped me up.

We surveyed the northern shepherds' fenrir trap. It gave off creepy druid vibes. A quarter mile away, Sertalis towered over a four-foot stake that had been driven into the earth. The pole had been carved with forearm-sized sigils, shiny and metallic. The amp ward. Here and there in the distance, I spotted gray-robed shepherds, creating a ridiculously wide perimeter around him.

"What are you doing here?"

Of course it was Darby who spotted us first. She'd at least given her hair some love since the last I'd seen her, platinum ringlets back to their salon-quality sheen. She couldn't wash away the stress lines on her face, though.

Guntram stiffened so hard, I worried he'd snap. "We're here to talk you out of this madness."

Darby clenched her jaw. "And why is that? So you can save face?"

Guntram rounded on her so fast, I worried he would strike her. "You, of all shepherds, should know better than to lay a trap here. Tabitha's spirit could be exposed along with Nasci's lifeblood!"

Darby clenched her jaw, her body so rigid it might snap. "The Oracle doesn't seem to mind. You can plead to her again, if you wish. She's up there keeping watch."

We couldn't see anyone in the boulder patch where Darby was pointing, but a pair of blue jays circling overhead indicated the Oracle was indeed nearby.

Guntram scowled. "You could have at least staked a different face of the mountain. This is exactly where we fought Rafe."

Guntram was right. I remembered Zibel tumbling down the ridge right next to my boots. The pole would have been very close to where Tabitha had sacrificed herself to the magma.

But Darby didn't care. "Elif didn't sense a drop of Nasci's lifeblood when she set up the ward, but she said this place would serve us best. Even more impressive, Elif discovered a rare metal that can mask Nasci's scent. That's why she's carved her sigils using that substance."

"You mean tungsten?" I asked, even though from how

similar the ward looked to Sipho's, I already knew the answer.

Darby nodded. "With it, she's confident the fenrir will never sense the old wound, even if we are right on top of it. In fact, doing so allowed her to boost the ward's aura. If the fenrir is anywhere near the Columbia River Gorge, he'll come."

"It's not enough. Sipho's been using tungsten for a while to create damp wards. Tungsten will still leak lifeblood without a fiberglass coating. If the fenrir senses it—"

"What ridiculous objections!" Darby cut me off with a mocking laugh. "No offense, haggard, but Sipho is a mere shadow of a forger compared to Elif. She probably can't create a proper ward because it's simply beyond her ability."

I didn't have time to argue as a sharp whistle cut through the air, echoing as it traveled from beyond our sight to reach us. Several more followed from roughly the same direction. Sertalis reacted by spreading his feet apart and igniting fire at his fingertips.

"The fenrir is near." Darby jumped back over the ridge, using earth sigils to stick to the rock face and peek over with her head. "Get out of sight. The last thing we need is for two southern shepherds to ruin our entire plan by distracting the fenrir."

Although Guntram looked like he'd swallowed a sea urchin, spines and all, he ducked behind the rock wall. I reluctantly did the same.

I used my free elbow to jab Darby in the ribs. "This is your great plan? Have Sertalis act as bait until the fenrir shows up and have everyone attack it?"

"Not everyone. Just Sertalis. He just needs one clean shot. The rest of us will augment the Oracle's elemental barrier, so the fenrir will not escape. He should have plenty of time even if it takes a strike or two."

"I'm not worrying about the fenrir escaping," I said,

remembering how fast it moved back at Sherman Creek. "I'm worried about it mauling someone."

"Shush," Guntram quieted us both. "The fenrir approaches."

The wolf vaettur appeared directly opposite us, appearing small on the curved mountain horizon. It grew larger as it leaped like an Olympic hurdler across the slopes, the lattice lights woven into its fur blinking in rhythm to its pace. The fenrir didn't notice Sertalis until it came within a city block of the amp ward. It skidded to a stop, lifted its head, and howled, a sound that echoed across the valley.

Darby gasped and shrank into herself. Yeah, girl. Same.

A sharp breeze tickled me from Guntram's direction. "Why doesn't Sertalis attack?" he asked in a harsh whisper.

"Sertalis will give the signal," Darby replied even softer. "Then the Oracle will activate the barrier."

The fenrir raised its hackles, taking purposeful steps toward the fire augur. Slowly, it closed the distance by half. Sertalis just stood there, waiting in his sigil stance.

The breeze intensified to a heavy gust. "The arrogant fool should strike now," Guntram mumbled.

Apparently, the Oracle agreed because despite Sertalis not giving the signal, a shimmering haze suddenly erupted upslope near the boulders. It spread out as a dome, washing over us in an elemental wave of pith. It felt like stepping into a hot spring, all that energy pushing against my pithways. Guntram directed his angry wind into the dome. Darby did the same with earth sigils. I fed it a simple water splash. Our three elements added to the barrier as it encompassed the entire mountainside, sparkling wherever it touched a gray robed figure feeding it pith.

The fenrir sensed the makeshift prison around it, snarling and whipping about in all directions.

Sertalis glared up the mountain but finally made his move. He morphed into a man of fire. The details of his body became lost as the flames swirled around him in a circular swoosh, the air currents creating a haze at the tips. In this superman form, he drew a five-pointed star. Flames streamed off of him in a whiplash arc, heading straight for the fenrir. The entire attack from start to finish took less than a heartbeat.

The fenrir screamed as flames surrounded it, then went eerily silent. A direct hit.

"Yes," Darby said.

It all seemed so anti-climactic. I pushed myself upward onto the ledge. "At least it's over and done."

But Guntram yanked me back down. "Wait."

The terror in his voice made my pulse quicken. I ducked back down, but I couldn't see either Sertalis or the fenrir through the smoke trails left by attack. "It didn't take?"

"No," he said.

"You jealous old man," Darby scolded as she jumped up to the ledge. "Just because Sertalis defeated the fenrir after you failed—"

A roar of fury worthy of the Jurassic age roared across Mt. Hood. The smoke parted to reveal Sertalis still standing there, back in human form with flames gone, staring at the smoldering earth where the fenrir had stood. It really did look like he'd banished it.

Until you noticed the massive wolf bearing down on him from the sky. The fenrir had leaped upward in a steep arc, aimed straight at Sertalis with claws extended.

Sertalis would have died right there if the earth under his feet hadn't flung him aside. As it was, he barely stumbled out of reach as the fenrir landed next to him. The lucky augur got a second break when Elif's pole fell and clocked the fenrir directly on the forehead. The fenrir shrieked in pain as Sertalis scrambled backward like a crab to create some distance between them.

"Thank Nasci for the Oracle." Guntram jumped over the ridge and ran toward the wolf. I followed before my brain could protest such a life-endangering move.

As we dashed forward, the fenrir crouched as if to pounce. I thought it would attack Sertalis, but something much more enticing had caught its attention. Instead, it dug into the dirt like a dog for a buried bone. The fallen ward's metal sigils suddenly glowed beside the fenrir with an intense light, like the sigils of Sipho's damp ward. The oppressive sensation in the atmosphere tripled.

Then the fenrir thrust its nose deep into the earth and swallowed. There was only one thing he could be consuming.

Nasci's lifeblood.

"No!" Guntram screamed.

The Oracle's elemental dome around us disappeared in a blink. That was all the warning she gave before she unleashed a landmine underneath the fenrir. The shockwaves from her earth sigil knocked both Guntram and me down. Soil coated my tongue.

A howling rushed toward us. I barely had time to register the enraged fenrir, covered in cuts and dirt from the explosion, bearing down on me before a gale knocked him aside. Guntram scrambled to his feet, his pupils lost in a white milkiness as he absorbed every last particle of air around him and drew a five-pointed star at the staggering fenrir.

Guntram had him dead to rights. He unleashed his air attack in a battle cry that made my ears ring.

Then the fenrir…vanished.

It didn't move. It didn't create a portal. It just blinked out of existence like a video game glitch.

Guntram's banishment sigil hit the ground where the fenrir had been, causing another whiplash of earth. I turned away to protect my face, which is how I saw the fenrir reappear right behind my mentor, teeth snapping to finish him off.

I cried out, searching for my lightning charm, but I didn't have time to use it. Guntram would be torn to pieces before I could so much as gather its energy into my pithways.

But the Oracle saved a second augur that day as a basketball-sized fireball slammed down between the fenrir and Guntram.

Smacked on the snout, the fenrir retreated a few steps as Guntram finally realized he'd almost become wolf dinner. Hands a blur, Guntram conjured a quick mini-tornado to slam into the fenrir, but the wolf executed another instant vanishing act before he could unleash it.

Guntram gaped at where the fenrir should have been. "What?"

"Jump!"

The Oracle's command sounded as if she'd shouted it from over my shoulder, but it was Guntram who literally flew into action. He shifted the tornado toward us so it blasted us up into the air. We swirled around in circles, rocketing to the top of the twister.

I was too disoriented to do anything useful spinning in the air, which is why I'm grateful Guntram handled easing our descent. I barely registered a hail of fireballs decimating the ground where we'd been, creating a rash of craters beneath my boots. At this high vantage point, I could see robed figures scurrying inward to lend magical assistance, shouting as they cleared the smoke with air sigils.

Guntram dropped us near the Oracle, also running toward the scene. Her white hair flew behind her, old joints as fluid as any professional sprinter in a 100-yard dash.

"Did you banish the fenrir?" Guntram called once she was within talking distance.

She shook her head, her eyes cold and hard. "No. It got away."

Guntram surveyed the pockmarked ground in disbelief. "But it was surrounded by shepherds! That's not possible."

"Anything is possible," she said grimly, "when a fenrir

can teleport.”

CHAPTER 21

WHILE MOST SHEPHERDS didn't have forger-like sensitivity, the Oracle's no ordinary shepherd. She informed us that Nasci's lifeblood now emanated from where we stood. The fenrir had cracked open a whole new lesion on the side of Mt. Hood.

Color me shocked. The northern shepherds had literally stuck a ward right over where Rafe had killed Tabitha to amplify the lesion scent. That's like sticking raw hamburger over a deer carcass and then wondering why scavengers ate the corpse. But the horrified faces of the gray-robed shepherds clearly indicated they hadn't expected this outcome.

Covered in bruises and dirt, Sertalis tried to justify his dumb plan to the others. "I almost had the fenrir. It leaped just above my fire banishment."

Guntram's beard bristled. "Close only counts in a game of horseshoes. You knew the fenrir would be wicked fast, and now it can move anywhere in the blink of an eye."

Sertalis glowered at him. "You think you could have done better?"

"I would not have attempted such foolishness in the first place. I warned all of you this could happen if you played around with the lesions."

Flames licked inside Sertalis's irises. "The lesions would not be a problem if the southern homestead hadn't created them."

"We did not create the lesions. Rafe did, after the northern homestead failed to stop him and left us to deal with the aftermath."

Sertalis rolled up his tunic sleeves. "Are we back to the duel then? Because I would gladly settle this once and for all right now."

"Enough!" The Oracle's booming voice alone would have caught our attention, but the waves of pure elemental energy she emitted made everyone wince. My pithways reacted like the world's worst tuning fork, vibrating in a way that made me itch all over, except I couldn't scratch inside my own body.

With a glowing halo reminiscent of wisp channel lights, she focused her unblinking gaze on Sertalis. "I thought I made it clear there was to be no duel with our current circumstances. Or did I miss you banishing the fenrir?"

Oh snap. I'd never seen the Oracle so enraged before. I'm not sure if I respected her more or if I wanted to run screaming, even though her anger wasn't directed at me.

Sertalis bowed his head, subdued for a change. "No, Oracle."

"Then I pray not to hear further talk of challenges. Otherwise, I will do something you will definitely regret. Do I make myself clear?"

"Yes, Oracle."

Satisfied with his submission, the Oracle shifted to address the rest of us. The gray robes all took an unconscious step back. Even Darby's chin wilted a little. Only Guntram remained unaffected, his spine straight and tall.

"Against my better judgment, I authorized this plan of attack, and thus I take full responsibility for the outcome. It is as Guntram warned us. The fenrir absorbed magma. It now has infinite speed with the ability to teleport at will within our world."

"And it will come back for more," Guntram said.

"Agreed," she said. "The fenrir cannot ingest another bite. We can no longer afford to be divided. We must band together to guard all the lesions. To that end, I put Guntram in charge of allocating all Talol Wilds shepherds to guard duty so that each lesion is covered by multiple shepherds around the clock."

Sertalis's head snapped up at this, clearly unhappy, but he wisely kept his mouth shut.

"You should know that Sipho has a working prototype of a damp ward that may seal the lesion completely," Guntram told her. "If we can give her more time to refine it, we might not need the guards anymore."

The Oracle nodded. "I would like to visit her soon and view her work."

"Why not right away?" I blurted out, not meaning to sound pushy, but it came out that way just the same. Gray hoods turned to stare daggers at me.

The Oracle, however, did not get upset with my question. Instead, she bent over the broken pole Elif had made, stroking the dark wood with her fingertips. "Because I must first figure out how to banish the fenrir."

Sertalis's humility vanished once it appeared the Oracle might make decisions without him. "I could work with you on that. I have other strategies to consider."

The Oracle shook her head. "I heard all your proposals back at the amphitheater. Unfortunately, they all rely on the same thing."

Sertalis's brow wrinkled. "Please explain."

She stood, frowning at the amp ward. "You believe we can banish this fenrir using conventional means. Earth. Fire. Air. Water. And yet we tried that, even before the fenrir absorbed Nasci's lifeblood. It was too quick for us then, and any of those methods will be impossible now."

Sertalis stiffened. "We've only tried fire. The other

elements could still banish it.”

The frown on the Oracle’s face could have withered fresh wildflowers. “You forget that Guntram, master of air, also attempted to banish the fenrir. Were you knocked too silly to see that?”

Damn, the Oracle really wasn’t pulling any punches.

A few incoherent syllables came out of Sertalis’s lips. “Guntram is injured,” he finally settled on. “Surely someone in peak form, such as yourself, could have executed a proper five-pointed star.”

Proper? I took a step forward, mouth open to tell Sertalis where he could shove his criticism of Guntram’s abilities. If my mentor hadn’t laid a hand on my shoulder to shut me up, I’m sure I would have said something nasty.

And besides, Yoi had it covered. “What makes you think I didn’t try to banish the fenrir?”

The implication sent a shiver through the crowd. Sertalis paled. “You can’t be serious.”

“Do I look like I’m joking?” The Oracle sighed. “I tried several times after the fenrir ingested Nasci’s lifeblood, to no avail. Every time I’d get halfway through a five-pointed star, the fenrir had moved so fast I could barely keep up. A fenrir banishment requires strict target control, and with its normal speed combined with teleportation, I could not predict where to send my magic.”

The audience shiver morphed into audible gasps, myself included. No one wanted to hear that the Oracle couldn’t banish a vaettur. That was the stuff right out of shepherd nightmares.

One of the gray robes called out, “Then we are doomed!”

“No, we find something faster. Something the fenrir cannot hope to outrun.” She turned straight to me. “Like lightning.”

I’m pretty sure time stood still. No one moved, not even a muscle. Definitely not me, the object of the Oracle’s declaration. She thought I was going to banish the fenrir? After two augurs and she herself had failed?

Shouts of dismay went up in the crowd. Everyone started talking at once, Sertalis the loudest of all. Even so, you couldn't make out a single coherent sentence, just bits and pieces of argument and outrage.

"…too young…"

"…unstable magic…"

"…haggard…"

Basically, the greatest hits of every criticism I'd ever heard since I began my eyas training.

The Oracle lifted her foot and lightly tapped the ground. No visible sigil writing, no dramatic stomp, just a toe-tapping as if keeping the rhythm to her favorite song. It resulted in a ripple wave of earth that spread out from her in concentric circles, rocks bouncing to knock us in the navel. A few earth shepherds like Darby managed to write a rapid countersigil to keep themselves upright while the rest of us danced on unsteady ground.

"I am not requesting input from any of you," she declared as calmly as a math teacher assigns extra homework to a whiny class. "Ina will come with me while the rest of you confer with Guntram about when and where to guard the lesions for the next few days. Do I make myself clear?"

She took the reluctant mumbling as agreement, then lifted her fingers toward me. "If you would walk with me?"

I gulped, wondering what the Oracle had signed me up for. Don't get me wrong, I liked a vote of confidence as much as the next shepherd, but a part of me agreed with the peanut gallery.

How was I going to stop a fenrir?

CHAPTER 22

THE ORACLE LED me away from the commotion on Mt. Hood toward the nearest wisp channel. We teleported to the Washington side of the Columbia River, high enough up to watch car lights shine on the southern freeway. I waited for the Oracle to tell me about her big plan, but nope, she said nothing as we hiked up a slope. I had to jog to keep up with her spry moves.

She looked like she should be browsing nursing home brochures, and she could outmaneuver me. Wonderful blow to my ego.

We went through a second wisp channel, leading us farther north into the Cascades before I could no longer keep quiet.

"You really think I can banish a fenrir?"

"No." Her answer came out so swift and sure, I almost stumbled on a root. "But you're the only option we have."

I couldn't control my sudden anger. "Look, I get that older shepherds love the whole tough love thing, but this goes way beyond Guntram burying me up to my neck in earth and telling me to claw my way out. I'm going to need a little more reassurance if you want me to do this."

She halted in her tracks. "You'd defy the Oracle?"

I was proud of myself for stifling my gulp. Still, I was done with the cryptic crud. "Yes. Absolutely. You know me by now, right?"

I didn't expect her to take that well, but her expression softened. "Indeed. That is exactly why I believe this even has a chance of working."

She resumed walking, so I tentatively followed.

"What do you know about your lightning pith, Ina?"

"I'm the only one who has it," I answered glibly.

"Try to answer without the sarcasm this time."

Okay, that was fair. I dissected what I'd learned about my unique pith over the last year. "Lightning hurts too much to store in my pithways. I have to rely on my charm for pith."

"Anything else?"

What did she want me to say? "It tends to pop up around the weird fox dryant I can't find."

"Ah yes." Her satisfied reply told me I'd found the answer she sought. "The mysterious dryant."

"Others have seen it," I said, suddenly defensive about this sore issue. "Everyone in the southern homestead, and even Wuaro." Then I slapped my hand over my mouth. She didn't know how I'd wandered onto Bitai Wilds land without permission, and therefore, wouldn't know I'd made friends with one of their shepherds.

Then she proved me wrong. "I've been appraised of your excursions into the Bitai Wilds, but that is neither here nor there. Don't you find it curious that the fox only ever shows up when you're around?"

"I don't know what to think about the fox," I said honestly. "Except..." But maybe I shouldn't mention any weird family history.

Too late. The Oracle motioned for me to continue.

"It may be a Japanese fairy tale, but my dad mentioned that kitsune possession runs in the family. Kitsune are basically supernatural foxes. One supposedly possessed my grandma's sister. She could see ghosts and talk to animals."

"Sounds like ken to me."

"I thought so too, but I'm not sure what to make of it. Dryants don't live inside people. They guard other animals."

"Are you sure about that?"

I nearly choked on air. "Are you saying my great aunt had a fox dryant living inside her?"

"I have no concrete way of verifying it, but it may well be the case."

I halted again. "How long have you known?"

The Oracle patted me gently on the shoulder. "I have suspected for a very long time. The unusual circumstances of your Shepherd Trial cemented the idea in my mind."

That left one nagging problem. "If I had a dryant living inside me, why didn't you tell the others?"

"Such relationships between shepherds and dryants are exceedingly rare here in the Talol Wilds and even throughout the continent. The others wouldn't have believed me even if I'd told them."

Suddenly, the whole fiasco that the Oracle had put me through to find the fox dryant made sense. "You wanted me to summon the kitsune to prove its existence."

She nodded. "I've heard shepherds with such abilities are often able to do so."

As charming as the Oracle could be, I could have slapped her at that moment if her return punch wouldn't have stung harder. "Then why didn't you say anything? I spent the week running around like the world's biggest idiot when I could have been spending that time trying to summon it from inside me!"

She gave me a conspiratorial smile. "Because most things are better learned through experience than lecture. You will internalize the knowledge more naturally to your advantage."

That nugget of wisdom held a deep flaw. "Except my dad is the one who told me about the kitsune. I wouldn't have figured it out on my own."

"I disagree. Your father merely planted a seed. You're the one who made the connection between that conversation and this possible truth about your abilities. And it can only be you who figures out how to summon the dryant. In that, I could not help you even if I wanted to."

I tried to make sense of what this had to do with our current disaster. "Maybe we're looking at this the wrong way. What about Tabitha? She managed to banish a fenrir singlehandedly. Why don't we do whatever she did last time?"

"Even if the fenrir hadn't gained the ability to teleport, I'm afraid that's not possible."

"Why?" My unasked question, why does this have to fall on me?

"Because while her feat was legendary, the execution was more luck than skill. You see, Tabitha went berserk when her eyas Phineas died under the claws of the fenrir. Instead of fleeing for a ranged attack, the best strategy when dealing with a fenrir, she dove toward it. The move should have gotten her killed. In fact, the fenrir did manage to slice open her belly."

My pulse raced. I'd never heard this story. "And Tabitha survived?"

"Barely. And only because she was standing next to a cliffside and toppled it onto the fenrir did she manage even that. Her kidama deer led us to her, hanging onto life by a thread. It's only through Nasci's divine will she survived at all, and it still took her months to recover."

Whoa. I knew Tabitha had earth chops, but moving a construction site's worth of dirt would take me some effort. I couldn't imagine knocking over an entire cliff, no matter how small. And I certainly couldn't do it with a fenrir snacking on me.

"Yeah, I get your point. Tabitha's route doesn't seem like something we can repeat."

The Oracle's cheeks crinkled with worry. "It is a lot to

ask of you, but I see no other solution than your lightning. I will do my utmost to support you every step of the way. First, I will ask Elif if she can make another amp ward to attract the vaettur. Rest and come to the northern homestead tomorrow to check if it's done. Once the ward is made, we will devise a plan for how to use it."

I nodded, understanding the need for bait. "And what should I do until then?"

She pointed at my battery-powered lightning charm. "Guntram told me that doesn't hold a lot of pith."

"It gives me one good shot. Maybe two if I'm lucky."

"That gives you very little room for error when you face the fenrir. Determine if you can find another way to wield lightning."

The world seemed to spin a bit around me as I understood what she asked of me. "You want me to figure out how to summon the fox dryant? Overnight?"

"If possible. For when the time comes, it may be the razor thin advantage that separates you from death."

CHAPTER 23

IT'S A GOOD thing the Oracle didn't ask the impossible of me. Otherwise, I'd be in big trouble.

Even my internal sarcasm didn't help diminish my growing fear after the Oracle left. What she'd said made sense. If I could figure out how to summon the fox dryant, I'd have a constant source of lightning pith. It might be enough to take down a fenrir that could teleport at will.

But how on Nasci's green earth was I supposed to do that?

My poor brain was mush by that point, so I decided to get rest. I returned to Sipho's homestead near dark, grabbing a new defensive charm out of an empty forge and then taking a dip in the hot spring. Then I crashed harder than a frat boy on New Year's Day, even though it was well before midnight.

Because of my early bedtime, I accomplished the unthinkable the next morning: I actually got up voluntarily before eight o'clock. Much as I wanted to avoid it, my mind refused to let go of my current dilemma: how to summon the fox dryant.

With no real clue how to proceed, I could only search where it all began, the desert plains where I'd first learned to control lightning. While technically outside my permitted territory, the Oracle hadn't seemed upset that I'd been to the Bitai Wilds before on my own. Anything that could help me jumpstart my search had to be better than nothing.

So after a quick breakfast of berries and dried salmon (don't knock it, it actually tasted delicious), I wisped through fields of flowers and mountain vistas. I soaked in ambient pith to calm myself. Energy flowed in and out of my skin via osmosis. The chirping birds and fresh new day only added to my resolve.

I could do this. I had to do this.

Before wandering onto the flat sagebrush lands of the Bitai, I left my phone under a familiar rock near Derrick Cave, hoping to spare its sensitive electronics a lightning strike. Before powering it down, I found an old text message from Vincent, saying he would likely be discharged tonight. I must have slept so hard, I missed it. I thought about replying, but I didn't have the guts to tell him I was going to throw myself in front of a fenrir with little else besides a hope and a prayer. Instead, I took the coward's route and hid the phone away.

As the trees disappeared behind me to the west, I hoped to run into Wuaro. He might not be able to help me with the fox dryant, but I would have felt less lonely with him nearby. I even called out his name, my echo startling a couple of jackrabbits.

Nope, no Wuaro. I was on my own.

I stared up at the endlessly bright blue sky, not a cloud in sight on this breezeless day. "Time to pull a dryant out of my body!" I declared to no one. I almost said 'out of my butt' before deciding not to be so crude, although if I were honest, I would have been relieved to conjure the fox out of any orifice.

How to do it? I closed my eyes and mentally patted down my pithways. Nothing felt different. I grabbed my lightning charm, its crackling warmth spreading through my arm.

"You in there, kitsune?" I murmured. "Come on out. I'd like to talk to you."

That worked about as well as you might expect, meaning it accomplished nothing. Grimacing, I allowed the lightning to push the other elements out of my pithways. I generally only do this when I'm desperate because it hurts, like having someone comb a hairbrush over the insides of your veins. Gritting my teeth, I held onto the lightning pith as best as I could.

"C'mon," I said, wiping sweat off my brow. "Where are you?"

Since nothing inside me seemed different, I cracked an eye open, praying to find gathering dark clouds in the sky. The fox dryant had always shown up with a storm. But nope, I stood like an idiot in the middle of a desert field, nary a breeze to cool my rising internal temperature.

I couldn't do this forever. Pith slipped out of my fingers, causing them to spark at the tips. "Listen here, fox! Get your furry tail out here!"

And that's when I finally lost my grip on my pithways.

When lightning rockets out of you with no direction, it's no bueno. It struck so fast that the force of it flung me backward. I watched it create a fan-like pattern of crackling energy as I flew farther and farther away. Gravity finally did its thing and discarded me in the middle of a sagebrush, where at least the plant cushioned any whiplash I might have experienced on a harder surface.

"Ouch," I moaned as I dragged myself out of the sharp leaves and branches, cutting my bare legs. I'd need two packages of bandages to cover all the small lines of blood. But worse than the outside wounds, my insides felt like they'd been wrung out and stretched over my aching skeletal system.

Despite all that, I reached for my lightning charm as I stood, hoping I had enough juice to try again. Unfortunately, I'd completely destroyed it with my first try.

That's what happened when I didn't try to control lightning properly. I couldn't even find the clasp that looped through the rest of my necklace.

"Perfect." I had to go back to Sipho's for another one. It honestly was just as well, since even writing a few simple water sigils to douse a small fire felt like torture.

This did not bode well for my odds on banishing a freaking fenrir.

* * *

You know your goddess has a sense of humor when she piles on the pain when you're already down. How else do I explain that the first person I ran into on Sipho's homestead was Darby, who just happened to be on guard duty break and was soaking in the hot spring when I arrived. I even went to the forge first for a new lightning charm, and still no one was there. Darby's presence could have been random chance, but I like to think that the escalation of ridiculous circumstances had to be divine intervention at my expense.

Darby took one look at me from the confines of the steaming water and sneered. "The prodigal daughter returns."

"Stuff it, Darbs." I stripped off my slightly singed hoodie and flung it at her. She dodged it, the fabric missing her face by inches. The hoodie sank under the water, but it was totally worth the sigils to dry it off later.

"So mature," she said as I quickly got undressed and slid into the pool near the entrance, as far away from her as possible. I could have walked down to the lower pool, but that involved stairs, and they were my worst enemy after the painful hike back from the desert.

"This is how much I care about maturity," I said, not even bothering to make space between my pinching finger and thumb. There was probably an atom in there somewhere.

162

"And joking in the middle of a crisis," she said. "Is that how you're going to save us? With your witty banter?"

"The Oracle asked me to summon the lightning fox dryant."

Darby huffed. "You mean, the one you couldn't find because it doesn't actually exist?"

I gave her a good long stare. "The Oracle believes the fox lives inside me."

Darby gaped at me in disbelief. She'd been the one to file a petition against me to find the fox dryant, hoping my failure would revoke my shepherd status. No one (besides the Oracle apparently) had dreamed it might be because the fox was somehow a part of me.

"That is the most ridiculous thing I've ever heard," Darby declared. "And that's saying a lot with you. How did you convince the Oracle of such utter nonsense?"

"I didn't convince her at all. She's the one trying to get me to believe it."

Darby grabbed onto the pool's rocky edge so tightly, her knuckles turned white. "If that's true, why didn't you summon your little fox friend during my petition and save yourself?"

I knew how bad it would sound, but I'd started down this path. "Because I don't know how to do it."

"Of course!" Darby threw her hands up in the air. "That's the way it always is with you. Special rules. The gifted child that can do no wrong."

"I've done plenty wrong, Darby. I don't claim to be perfect. I'm just trying to protect Nasci like the rest of us."

"Then why are you fiddling around here taking a bath when you could be out there saving us, oh great lightning shepherd?"

I shrugged underneath the water. "I'm waiting on Elif."

"Elif's working with you?" Darby looked like I'd told her the sun circled the moon.

"The Oracle asked Elif to create another amp ward to bait the fenrir."

Darby huffed into the water. "At least the Oracle still has the sense to ask Elif for help where Sipho has failed."

Fire pith from the magma-fueled waters burst into my pithways. I could stand Darby taking pot shots at me all day, but it really rankled when she started in on Sipho. "Like you're doing anything important hanging around here, Darby. Don't you have a lesion to be guarding? You know, something actually useful?"

The water's surface rippled with mini tremors. "Don't you talk to me about lesions. They're all your fault. I expect one to form near the Columbia any day now."

So typical. She could dish it out but never take it. "Why? Because everyone's out to get you?"

"Because it fits the pattern!" she snarled. "All the spots where Rafe ripped open the earth are becoming lesions. Mt. Hood, the Gorge, the coast…It's only a matter of time before the entire Talol Wilds is marred by the scars of your utter failure."

I wanted to argue with her, but she had a point. A lot of this did lead back to me, even if I'd tried to forgive myself for it. I sighed. "How many times do you and I have to go over this? You're the one who dropped the petition to have me bound because Tabitha spoke to you in a vision. Doesn't that mean anything?"

"It's exactly because I know Tabitha's in there that I can't let it go!"

I squinted at her vehemence. "What are you even talking about?"

"Don't act dumb! How else do you explain the deer?"

She radiated so much raw earth pith that I squirmed on the stone bench. "You mean the ones that hang around the lesions?"

"They're Tabitha's old kidama! They guard her spirit, still trapped in Nasci's lifeblood. Guntram knows it too. He keeps saying Tabitha's spirit will pass on once we seal the lesions, and yet here we are. Months later, and Tabitha remains unable to pass properly back into Nasci."

"Sipho's been trying to seal the lesions."

"She's failed! I wanted Elif to get involved after it took so long, but Guntram asked me to give the south a chance to work things out. I'm tired of waiting while Tabitha suffers. I had to do something, and Sertalis was the only one who would even listen to me." Her chest heaved, and I could tell she was on the verge of tears.

And there it was. The reason why Darby had narked on us. I'd always assumed it had been a beef against me gone too far, but it was worse than that. She felt the whole southern homestead had betrayed her.

And a small part of me understood.

"I get it," I tried to reason with her. "It's hard to sacrifice as much as you have."

But Darby had already gotten to her feet, striding across the pool to leave. "You understand nothing about sacrifice. Everything has always been handed to you, and you have everyone's full support."

I gave her a wide berth as I snorted. "That's a very delusional way to look at things. Especially since your own augur tried to get me bound pretty much my entire time as an eyas."

Darby slipped into a generic gray robe she had folded on a boulder beyond the pool's edge. She flashed me a glare as she straightened the wrinkles out. "Sertalis understands. He knows you for what you are, a complete sham to all who follow Nasci."

"Sertalis is using you to get complete control of both homesteads, the exact opposite of what Tabitha would have wanted."

Darby drew an earth sigil so fast I barely had time to recognize the boulder that had held her clothes hurtling toward me. I managed to throw myself out of the way before getting crushed, the rock smashing hard into the water where I'd been sitting.

"Don't throw things at me ever again," Darby called over her shoulder as she stormed away from the hot spring.

CHAPTER 24

DARBY SURE HAD a way with rocks. I leaned my back against the boulder that had nearly flattened me and sank deeper into the water. I suppose I should have felt more threatened, but I was too sore, and besides, it let me lean my head back at the perfect angle to relax. That's how I roll: turning death threats into spa treatment.

My pithways slowly eased as fresh elements flowed through them. Although the hot spring eased the minor aches and cuts, it could not stem the heavy burden of responsibility. Somehow, I needed to access the fox dryant or risk losing it all against the fenrir.

As much as I love running into situations that could get me killed, this one seemed even more reckless than most. I knew that the fenrir could not only move faster than anything I'd ever fought on record, it could now freaking teleport. There's a reason the speedster characters in superhero movies are always ridiculously overpowered. It doesn't matter if you're impervious to bullets or can punch a hole in a skyscraper, if you can't catch your opponent, you're screwed.

"How do you stop something like that?" I asked the steaming water.

A repetitive quacking caught my attention. My phone had fallen partway out of my hoodie's kangaroo pouch. The screen lit up with a call, the bold letters "VIN" clear even at this distance.

Comfortable and lazy, I wrote a series of sigils that jostled the pebbles underneath the phone to send it skidding toward me. Magic powers aren't just for fighting otherworldly monsters.

I brought the phone to my ear and answered. "Heya."

"Back at you. Did you get my earlier message?"

"That you're getting discharged tonight? That's great news."

He rushed into his next words. "I'm so sorry about my mom. There's no excuse for any of her behavior."

His remorse was so painfully clear, but I decided he deserved to squirm a bit. "I thought you wanted your mom to like me."

"I do, but not enough to lose you. I meant it when I told her you're my girlfriend. I won't let her get between us. Are you still upset? Because you have every right to be. I can disown the whole lot of them. Please just—"

I couldn't let him go on. "You don't have to disown anyone. I'm fine. We're fine."

"Really?" he sounded so adorably hopeful.

"It's not like there's a line forming anywhere to date me. Besides, I have bigger problems on my hand."

A dark undertone entered Vincent's voice. "The fenrir."

"Yes, the fenrir." I hesitated to tell him the current plan, but he deserved the truth. "The northern shepherds tried to banish it and failed. Worse, it created a new lesion on Mt. Hood and can teleport now."

"T-teleport?" Vincent squeaked.

"Yeah, it's bad. The Oracle believes I'm the only one who can stop it now. She's figuring out a way to lure it out in the open so I can zap it with lightning." I tried to keep my voice cheerful, but a waver crept in anyway. "There's a good chance I'll miss and be dog meat, but she doesn't think there's any option even worth trying."

I took a deep breath, intending to explain the Oracle's kitsune theory, when Vincent's desperate plea interrupted me. "Ina, you can't face that thing."

I immediately went into defensive mode. "I'm a shepherd. It's what I do."

"I don't care," he snapped.

"You don't get to decide what—"

"It will kill you!"

I couldn't argue. I'd just been thinking the same thing myself.

"Someone has to stop it," I said on a choke. "What else can I do?"

"Wait," Vincent said, sounding as if his brain cells were firing on all cylinders. "You said it can teleport?"

"Yes?" I had no idea where he was going with the conversation.

"I can help!" he exclaimed with fierce determination.

"Vince, I know you're concerned, but—"

"No, listen. I can grab onto it with my magic. You know I can do it. You saw me back at the pickup truck."

My face flushed and not because of the hot water. Vincent had indeed frozen the fenrir before. But he was also an innate with no proper training. "Vince," I warned.

But he'd clearly warmed up to the idea. "If I can immobilize it, you can strike it with lightning, right?"

"Are you the same guy I've been dating these past few months? What happened to the guy who insisted he didn't have magic?"

"He finally got some sense knocked into him. And I'm not letting go. I can do this."

"You could get hurt," I argued.

"So could you! Ina, don't shut me out here, please."

"I'm not trying to shut anyone out. I just can't let you…" I couldn't finish my sentence.

"…let you die?" he finished for me. His voice broke as

he added, "And you think I'd let you do the same, especially if I could have helped?"

He had a point, but my heart searched for a way out of this solution. Vincent had just recovered from his first fenrir attack. He deserved a break. This wasn't his fight.

Except I knew, if the situation were reversed, it would break me if I didn't at least try.

"You still there?" he asked as my mind went into overdrive.

"Yeah. I'm thinking. I understand where you're coming from—"

"Great, then come up here and get me."

I hesitated. "I don't know."

He latched onto the cracks in my armor. "Great. I won't leave the hospital without you. See you in a couple hours, tops."

And then he hung up on me.

* * *

I could have been mad, but I routinely cut off calls when I want to make a point. Vincent had made his. And despite the dread I felt at Vincent confronting the fenrir with his untested magic, I couldn't deny the equally powerful glimmer of hope.

Maybe I didn't need the fox dryant. Vincent might give me the edge to blast wolfie back to Letum with lightning.

Those warring emotions made the scenery blend into a blur, through wisp channels, past woods, and straight into Colville. The golf course and suburban neighborhoods whizzed by. Skipping the receptionist and heading straight for Vincent's wing, I was so focused on my shepherd mission that I never considered the more immediate danger I faced.

I stepped into Vincent's room and found Teresa, her back to me as she looked out the window. I froze like a paleontologist suddenly confronted with a live T-Rex, trying not to make any sudden moves to alert her to my presence. I noticed her slumped shoulders and the tissue clenched in her hand. She sniffled loudly, confirming my worse suspicions.

She'd been crying.

I slowly backed away, inching toward my escape. I thought I'd made it when a friendly voice called out to me from the hallway.

"Ina!" Vincent said, dressed in a clean T-shirt and jeans with a huge smile on his face. He looked a thousand percent better from when I'd last seen him. "You made it!"

I waved my hands to shush him, but it was too late. Teresa snapped around, and if her gaze had carried any physical weight, it would have knocked me to the floor. She slapped her cheeks a couple of times with the tissue and then tossed it into a garbage can. Gone were any lingering tears, replaced by the righteous fury of an angel. She was only missing wings and a heavenly light to blind me permanently.

"You again," she snarled. "What are you doing here?"

Vincent, realizing what he had done, hurried to put himself between us. "Mom, what are you doing here? I thought you'd left with everyone else."

"I'm your mother. Since you wouldn't tell me where you were going after you got discharged, I decided to stay." Her expression intensified as she stared straight at me. "It's a good thing, too, now that she's come back."

I opened my mouth to retort, but Vincent spoke first. "Mom, Ina's here because I asked her to come. You will treat her with respect."

"She's evil."

"Oh please," I rolled my eyes.

Teresa scowled. "You see. There she goes again. Acting as if a mother's concern for her son's well-being means absolutely nothing."

Vincent cursed under his breath. "I get that you're worried about me, but the doctor says I'm fine. You didn't think anything of it until I told you I wasn't going home with the rest of the family."

"It's where you belong!" She tapped a high heel, and a slight tremor rumbled across the floor. I crouched a little, prepared to draw a countersigil if she released any more magic. I don't even know if she realized what she was doing.

"I'm still part of the family," Vincent replied. "I'm just dating Ina now. Get used to it."

"But Christy—"

"Cheated on me, Mom! Broke my heart! It's done. Over. You need to let it go."

"Maybe I could do that, but with her?" She pointed at me with contempt. The tremors spiked. I wrote half a square, ready to stop Teresa from harming anyone.

But I didn't have to finish. Vincent took an aggressive step forward and towered over his mother. All the earth pith radiating off Teresa just stopped.

Teresa clenched her fists, but nothing changed. "Wh-what is this?" She gasped.

Vincent took a deep breath before saying. "It's magic, Mom. My magic."

Whoa. He'd admitted it. And to his mom.

Teresa looked equally gobsmacked. "This…this can't be real."

"Isn't that what you always wanted? Aren't you proud?"

Teresa held her ground for a few seconds before she crumpled, new tears streaming down her face. "So you're siding with…her? You hate your own family so much?"

"No, Mom. I just make my own decisions. Even ones that you don't like."

But she kept babbling to herself as she snatched her purse off a nearby counter. "I knew she was trouble the minute I saw her. She's taking you away from us."

Poor Vincent ran his fingers through his hair. "She made me believe in magic. Why doesn't that make you happy?”

She stormed toward the doorway but paused to fling back the last word. “I warn you, Vincente. This woman is not one of us. She is one of the monsters. And if you are not careful, she will consume you.”

Then she stormed off. Vincent simply stared after where she’d last been, his posture slack with sadness.

“I’m so sorry,” I whispered. “I’m the one who caused her to act like that.” Some bridge between shepherds and the innates I was turning out to be. I was always going to be a constant source of drama.

Vincent flipped around, clasping my shoulders. “You’re not responsible for my mother’s actions. If anything, I’m the jackass that pushed you away.”

“I’m always walking into situations and making things worse.”

“You saved me from the fenrir. I’d be dead if not for you.”

“The day is young, Vince. I still have time to get you killed if you come with me.”

Vincent lifted my chin up, his fingertips burning fire pith along my jawline. I had little time to prepare as he gave me a long, hard kiss.

I have a lot of experience with heat, but I’m telling you, there is no element that makes my whole body sing like Vincent. My individual nerve endings soared. My knees went weak even though I felt like I could lift a building.

I leaned in for more.

When Vincent finally pulled away, he kept our noses touching at the tip. “Don’t you dare risk your life without me, Imogene Nakamori.”

“Okay,” I rasped. I probably would have agreed to anything he said at that moment.

He grinned from ear to ear at my lack of composure. “I’ll need to remember this trick next time I want you to agree with me.”

His smugness snapped me back to reality. My wagging

finger came between our faces. "Use your irresistible charm against me, Garcia, and I will electrocute you." I didn't really mean it, but somehow, without touching my lightning charm, an actual spark crackled on my fingertip.

Where had that come from?

We both took two steps back. "Point taken," Vincent said. "I'm at your mercy."

Embarrassed (and a little frightened) by my lack of control, I changed the subject. "We should get going. The Oracle expects me at the northern homestead soon."

Vincent gave an exaggerated bow. "Lead the way."

CHAPTER 25

UNLIKE ALL THE other times I'd traveled with Vincent, we couldn't take his Subaru. His family had supposedly taken it to a mechanic, but Vincent wasn't even sure which one. That left us with either trying to rent a car in this teeny, rural town or attempting more traditional shepherd travel.

I felt pretty confident Vincent could travel through wisp channels. It takes a lot of pith to travel through one, and he clearly had a heaping load if he could stop a fenrir in its tracks. Though a little reluctant, Vincent agreed to give it a shot.

The long hike gave me time to give Vincent a full recap of what had gone down on Mt. Hood. He tried to mask his anxiety over how the entire northern homestead had failed to banish the vaettur. Still, he didn't retract his offer to help me. If anything, he seemed more determined than ever before, threading his fingers through mine. We walked hand-in-hand the last few miles. I relaxed despite the dangers I knew lay ahead.

Past the golf course and into the woods came the moment of truth. Vincent spotted the twinkling blue lights before I did, a good sign, but he lingered at the tree's base before taking the plunge.

"What happens exactly?" Vincent asked.

"It's pretty basic. You step through. There's the briefest moment of being surrounded by the wisp lights. And then you come out somewhere else."

"It doesn't hurt?"

"It's agony," I said in a monotone. When he scowled at me, I threw up my hands. "C'mon, man, it'll be fine. Should I go first or you?"

He squeezed our enjoined hands. "Let's go together."

It was a cute sentiment but not practical since the wisp channel itself was a single-person doorway. I elbowed slightly ahead, holding onto Vincent's hand. I heard him gasp as the light overtook his vision, but he did not let go as I pulled him through.

Sometimes walking through a wisp channel doesn't feel so dramatic, since one forest can look like any other. We were in luck with this one, though, since we left a flatter meadow and emerged high on a ridge about ten miles southeast. All around us for 360 degrees spread a never-ending landscape of rolling pine trees, swaying under rushing clouds like ripples on a sea.

"Wow," Vincent breathed before taking in a sharp breath. The temperature had dropped significantly through the wisp channel.

I drew an inner heat sigil for me first, then wrote a second one on his cheek before he could ask what I was doing. He shivered as his fire pith ignited throughout his pithways, then stared down at his body in awe.

"You do that all the time?" he asked.

"How else do you think I stay warm with shorts on all year?"

"Magic." He shifted so the wisp channel lights danced in his eyes. "I can't believe it."

"Don't regress back to your grumpy old self now. We've got a big, bad wolf to evict from grandma's house."

As we dove into the tree line toward our next wisp

channel, I explained to Vincent that he couldn't come with me into the northern homestead. When he tried to argue, I told him the place had a guard wolverine that would rip him to shreds. This made him hesitate, and after I graphically described the fire techniques Sertalis might use to fry an intruder, he wisely acquiesced.

That's how I ended up alone back at the northern homestead. Like my previous visits, the place seemed deserted. I headed for the forge first, since that's where I was supposed to check on the ward. When I got there, smoke plumed from the curvy fortress to the sky, indicating someone was home.

I grabbed a metal knocker on the obsidian-etched front door and slammed it down.

Nothing.

I repeated the knock, adding for good measure, "Hello? Anyone home? You left your fireplace on."

Still no response.

Huh. Not even Quavik wanted a piece of me. Maybe I'd misinterpreted the Oracle's instructions and they really weren't home. I picked my way off the main path toward her longhouse. But that building was empty, a huge round boulder blocking the only circular entrance.

"Wonderful," I grumbled to myself as I trudged back toward the center of the homestead. "Now what am I supposed to do?"

Even though I wasn't expecting a reply, I got one. "Hello again, Ina the lightning shepherd!"

Oduvan appeared at the edge of a potato field, appearing no larger than a collie at this distance. She waved frantically with both arms and trotted toward me. I decided to meet her halfway. The closer we came through the rows, the more of her details emerged. She carried an enchanted hoe and was dirty from head-to-toe in a tunic with patched holes.

"Hey, Oduvan! Where is everyone?"

"Busy with the fenrir," she said, not winded in the least.

"I suppose that's why you're here."

I nodded. "I'm looking for Elif. Do you know where she is?"

"She should be at the forge. Is no one there?"

"It's shut up tight. No one answered when I knocked."

Oduvan shifted. "That's odd. I'm sure everyone's inside. They must be ignoring you."

What else was new with my life? "Who's everyone?"

"All the apprentices aiding Elif with forge work. We finished the second amp ward for the fenrir earlier today."

"Great! That's why I'm here."

Oduvan's cheerfulness wavered. "Are you sure you're the one who's supposed to pick it up, lass?"

I did not like the heavy ball that settled in the bottom of my stomach. "I thought so. The Oracle told me to come check and see if it's done."

Oduvan's brows suddenly creased in anger. "That's what I told Elif," she said in a near shout. "But Elif decided the Oracle wasn't clear on that point. That's why she gave the new ward to Sertalis."

My stomach ball grew spikes and rolled around, just for fun. "Sertalis is lugging around a large amp ward?"

She blinked in confusion before understanding lit her expression. "You're referring to the larger ward we made for Mt. Hood. We improved on the design for the second one. It might not pack as much punch, but it's smaller and easier to transport."

"But he still has it."

Oduvan reluctantly nodded. "Even though the Oracle told us it was for you, Sertalis showed up at the forge and insisted plans had changed. He said he would banish the fenrir. I protested when Elif handed it over to him, so she punished me with extra farm duties to remind me of my place. Then he left with that pretty blond earth shepherd an hour ago."

Darby. I'd told that little snitch about Elif's ward, and she'd run to tell big daddy Sertalis. I never thought in a million years she'd circumvent the Oracle's direct orders.

I tried to sympathize with Darby because I'd made similar calls in the past, but I couldn't. The Oracle didn't pick me because she was playing favorites. She believed lightning was our only chance at banishing the fenrir. Sertalis already had his chance. If he or Darby went after the fenrir again, especially now that it could teleport, they'd probably end up as shredded meat.

Maybe I could still stop them. "Do you have any idea where they went?"

Oduvan's brows scrunched together. "They didn't mention anywhere that I recall."

How was I supposed to track those two nutjobs down? I stifled a full-body sigh. "Thanks anyway, Oduvan. And I'm sorry you got in trouble for all this."

"It's not your fault. In fact, I'd hoped you'd come to set things right. Someone who offers to help a lowly apprentice with her chores can't be as bad as they say."

I flashed her a mischievous smile. "You could always refuse to harvest the fields."

"Someone must do the work, or the shepherds starve. Might as well be ol' Oduvan." She reached into a tunic pocket and withdrew a thin metal slat. "Here, take this. It might help."

I took the object from her. "A defensive charm?"

"One of my own designs. Don't get me wrong," she added quickly. "I always admired Sipho's craftsmanship. She had a knack for forging that makes even Elif a little jealous. But during a break yesterday at the forge, I had a flash of insight on how to adapt the basic defensive design to counteract the fenrir's physical strength and speed. I rarely have free time at the forge to pursue such ideas, but things were so frantic yesterday, I managed to sneak away and craft it."

"Thanks," I said. I already had a defensive charm of my own, but Vincent didn't. He'd broken his old one and would need the extra protection. "I appreciate this more than you know."

"Go with Nasci, and be safe. I don't want to hear of your passing, lightning shepherd."

* * *

My mind raced as fast as my feet as I backtracked to where I'd left Vincent. My best bet of tracking Darby and Sertalis down was to ask Guntram for help. He could send his kidama ravens as scouts to track them. Unfortunately, it would take precious time to return to the southern homestead, and even then, there was no guarantee Guntram would be there.

Part of me wondered if I should leave Darby and Sertalis to fight the fenrir by themselves. If they succeeded, I wouldn't have to go after it, and if they lost, it wouldn't be my fault. I pushed the thought aside. I'm not one to let people get themselves killed, even if they are complete morons.

Vincent must have heard me coming up the mountainside because he met me halfway down. He took one look at my face and asked, "What's wrong?"

I bent over, hands on my knees, to catch my breath. "Darby and Sertalis stole the amp ward."

Vincent stiffened. "I thought you and the Oracle were going to work together to catch the fenrir."

"That was the plan, but apparently it was too much for Sertalis's overinflated self-importance. Now I'm stuck trying to figure out where they went before they commit vaettur suicide trying to one-up me."

Vincent facepalmed. "Why is everything always so complicated with you?"

"Hey, it's not my fault that I'm so delightful."

He ignored my snark. "You don't have any clue where they could have gone? Maybe one of the lesion sites?"

"Those places are crawling with shepherds now. They wouldn't risk getting caught there."

180

"Where else could they lure the fenrir where the other shepherds wouldn't notice?"

"I don't know. I…" But then I paused. "Wait a minute. We're talking about the active lesion sites. What about the inactive ones?"

Vincent frowned. "I don't follow."

"The first amp ward lured the fenrir onto Mt. Hood. The northern shepherds chose that spot initially because it would spread a wide scent over the gorge, but the ward ended up tapping into an inactive lesion, where Rafe first accessed Nasci's lifeblood."

Vincent caught on. "If Darby and Sertalis take the amp ward to another former crevasse, they might be able to create a new hot spot as a trap."

"And Darby complained to me about a possible lesion forming where she patrols. I bet they went somewhere in the Columbia Gorge."

Vincent raised a skeptical eyebrow. "That barely narrows it down. You're still talking a hundred miles of river to cover."

I grabbed onto his bicep. "But we can narrow it down. Remember how we located the lesions in the first place? I used that earthquake database you have access to."

Vincent pulled out his phone. "If I log in and search for earthquakes that occurred in the Columbia Gorge during the time Rafe was running around, we should be able to find an old lesion site."

Of course, Vincent wasn't receiving cell reception, so we had to climb upslope to find a few bars first. Then Vincent clicked through a few websites and logged into his work accounts. Once he inputted all the parameters, there was only one location in the entire Columbia Gorge where unusual seismic activity had occurred during Rafe's brief reign of terror.

"Eagle Creek, south of Tunnel Falls," Vincent said. "Pretty remote, rugged terrain."

"Wisp channels can get us there." I was about to dash

off when I suddenly remembered the other thing I'd picked up at the northern homestead. "One more thing before we go. A little extra security." I handed Oduvan's defensive charm to Vincent.

Vincent took it gratefully. "The way things are going, I'm probably going to need it."

As we scrambled down the mountain, I hated thinking he was right.

CHAPTER 26

THE COLUMBIA RIVER Gorge is an outdoor enthusiast's dream. A canyon carved by the largest river in the Pacific Northwest, it cuts through the Cascade Mountains to forge dozens of breathtaking waterfalls over basalt cliffs. The surrounding forestland provides very little navigable paths due to dense bramble and steep inclines. We forged a path away from the river into these woods to find our inactive lesion. I even drew a square with a triangle in the middle of Vincent's hands so he could scramble on rocks he wouldn't otherwise be able to. Despite our urgency, I had to remind Vincent to keep moving every now and again because he'd pause at some majestic vista to stare.

"I can't believe this is your everyday view," Vincent said after one particular prodding.

"You're a park ranger. You should be used to this."

"I'm limited by forest service roads and places I can walk to. This is incredible."

I mean, he was right. "Maybe we'll come back and explore sometime."

"I'm holding you to it. It's a date."

I hid my happy blush with bluster. "You practice your

magic, and it's a deal."

All flirting faded as we approached the spot where Rafe had used an earthquake to tap into Nasci's lifeblood. Like Mt. Hood, something felt off about this place. The animals avoided the immediate underbrush, and that slasher vibe weighed down on me again.

Vincent picked up on it too. "Is it normally so quiet out here?"

"No." A shadow passed over us. Just clouds rolling over the sun. Still, it seemed less like chance and more like a warning.

The area itself was picturesque, the kind of place you'd want to pitch a tent if you could hike in that far. A rolling mountain stream cut through lush grasslands. A curtain of trunks imprisoned the glen, hemming us in. The stream itself flowed into a short waterfall downstream, offering a wide panorama of more green pine.

The only thing marring the image was the wide swatch of bare dirt in the center of the grass, as if a giant finger had gouged it out. Late wildflowers brushed our ankles as we approached. All the petaled heads had turned away from the dirt, as if repelled by its energy.

I bent over the dirt and used an earth sigil to thrust a few knuckles directly into the ground.

"Feel anything?" Vincent asked.

"Despite looking so out of place, nope, it feels ordinary to me. It's the general vibe of this place that feels wrong."

"So, what now?"

"I don't know. I guess I hoped we'd run into Sertalis and Darby, but it's not going to be that easy. Maybe we can—"

But apparently, I'd spoken too soon because the ground suddenly erupted underneath our feet.

I'd been buried alive so many times that I recognized the telltale sensation of bedrock scurrying away. I danced to the side and kept my footing, writing earth stabilizing sigils as I went. That's how I avoided getting swallowed up.

Vincent wasn't so lucky. He fell with a shriek, his entire body going under. Rocks skittered after him to close the gap quickly afterward.

"Vincent!" I threw myself on my knees, clawing where he had disappeared. He hadn't been standing directly on top of the lesion like I had, but he was close enough. What if magma lingered too close to the surface? He'd never survive. Drawing a flurry of squares, I attempted to release him from his stone prison.

Only the ground refused to budge.

In my sheer panic, I thought maybe I'd drawn the sigil wrong, but repeating the relatively simply shape had the same effect.

"You're beyond delusional if you think you can beat me with earth pith," a smug voice drifted over me.

"Darby!" I flipped around.

But of course, it was not just her but Sertalis as well. They slithered out of the forest shadows as surely as the augur's kidama garter snakes.

"Let him out!" I yelled at her, barely containing the urge to fry them both. "He doesn't have air down there."

An ugly scowl stole all of Darby's pretty features. "You're the one who brought a human into shepherd business. It would serve him right if he dies."

I didn't hold back then. I grabbed my lightning charm and let its sizzling pith take up my entire body. Then with a zigzag drawn in the air, I let it fly toward them.

But Darby and Sertalis had the advantage of premeditation. They'd guessed what I would do, and the instant I moved, they worked together to bring up a solid wall of earth between us. My lightning blasted into hard rock, creating a back spray of dust that shot back at me. I sputtered as I went momentarily blind.

More rumbling caused me to sink down to my ankles in earth. I was rooted to the spot. Struggling to maintain balance, I didn't register the hands clawing at my neck until it tore my entire charm necklace away from me. Then those same hands knocked me over, and if I hadn't freed myself with my last bit of stored earth pith, I probably would have broken an ankle in the subsequent fall. A heavy foot came down on my stomach, holding me in place.

As the dust cleared, Sertalis's golden-trimmed tunic came into view. He held my charm necklace above me in triumph. I didn't have a lot of pith left in my pithways, but anger pooled fire in my palms. I melted the cuff of my hoodie as I raised my hand up to my attacker.

Sertalis sneered at me. "First earth with Darby, and now you threaten me with fire? You're even more brainless than I thought possible."

"You disobeyed the Oracle's direct orders and stole the amp ward. Who're you calling brainless?"

"She'll understand once I banish the fenrir."

"And what about us? If you kill an innocent man or me with your pith, Nasci will know exactly what you've done."

Darby, who had come up behind Sertalis, froze with wide eyes. "She's right."

I could not take on both of them without my charm necklace, so I appealed to her. "I know you're angry, Darby, and you've lashed out a few times, but you're not a murderer."

Sertalis glowered at me. "You're trying to trick us, you little haggard."

I glowered right back. "I'm reminding you of the vows you took as a shepherd."

And to my utter relief, it worked. Even though Sertalis kept watch over me, Darby skirted to the side and wrote a series of earth sigils that brought Vincent back to the surface. I scrambled to reach him, but Sertalis put more pressure on his foot, pinning me down. I had to take Darby's word as she kneeled by Vincent's side and declared, "He's unconscious but breathing."

Sertalis threw Darby my charm necklace. "Whatever

you do, don't let her have that. The last thing we need is her foul lightning magic ruining this banishment."

"Lightning magic's the only thing that can take the fenrir out now. That's why the Oracle chose me for this job."

Sertalis's self-righteousness seemed to give him extra height as he towered above me. "The Oracle has been naive for too long. It started with splitting the Talol Wilds into two homesteads to appease the whims of a foreign augur. Guntram could not even control his eyas, but she allowed him leadership of half of our land. Her blatant favoritism only grew when she allowed him to train you, a haggard with loose morals and sacrilegious ken."

"And what about Tabitha?" I asked, hoping to reveal his true nature to Darby. "She followed the rules just fine, and she trusted Guntram."

He took the bait. "Tabitha was always too stubborn for her own good. I tried to break her out of it as head augur, but she refused to bend. The little traitor took the first opportunity to abandon her duty when she could."

Darby gasped. Sertalis shrank a little, realizing too late what he had said in front of Tabitha's biggest fan. "She might have come around eventually," he said without much conviction.

I couldn't help myself. I laughed. "Who's the liar now, Sertalis?"

A flash of heat spread from his bare toes into my chest. I attempted to absorb the fire pith, but I just didn't have his pithway capacity. I broke out in painful sweats as he continued to crush me, squirming desperately to get out from under his foothold.

"Sertalis?" Darby asked with a quiver.

"She needs to know her place," he hissed, but then he stepped off me. I curled up into a fetal ball, cycling the other elements in my pithways to soothe where it burned.

He crouched down, and his awful face became my whole field of vision. "I am banishing the fenrir. You will not interfere because if you attack us in any way, I will put you and your friend down. And not even Nasci will care if I do it in self-defense."

He gave me one last shove and then left me there. I didn't have the breath to argue. I also didn't have the magical chops to test his theory. Instead, I rolled on my back, catching a glimpse of the darkening clouds gathering above the tree crowns.

Sertalis stepped onto the bare dirt patch that marked the lesion. He removed a small cylindrical can with etchings on the side from his robe. The amp ward. He thrust it into the dirt, and a wave of putrid energy seeped into my pithways. I'd absorbed vaetturs before, and that had hurt, but this made my veins want to vomit. Callum called the energy coming out of the lesions 'bad mojo,' and I suddenly understood why as my magical senses screamed at me to run away. The etchings blinked to life so painfully bright, I had to look away.

Darby looked away and shuddered. "What is this horrid sensation?"

"It's the lesion," Sertalis said. "This ward, while not as powerful as the first, can interact directly with Nasci's lifeblood. Elif modified it so."

Darby paled. She knew that shepherds were never supposed to mess with Nasci's energy directly. "What?"

But Sertalis looked like a cat who'd cornered a mouse. "Don't worry. This is an excellent strategy for us. If the fenrir is anywhere in the gorge, this ward all but assures it will come here to us."

"And rip you to shreds," I finished. "C'mon, Darbs. This is epically insane. Don't go along with this."

She exploded a fist-sized rock next to my leg, pelting me so hard I'd have bruises tomorrow. Okay, got it. Zip it, Ina.

Sertalis hunkered down over the lesion, bunching up in a sigil stance and shifting constantly so he could survey all 360 degrees. This was a bad version of what happened last time on Mt. Hood. At least there he'd been out in the open surrounded by seasoned shepherds who had his back. Here beside the narrow stream, we were barricaded by forest that camouflaged anything creeping toward us. Plus, now the fenrir could teleport, so that made stalking us even easier.

Sertalis had made us all delicious targets for a hungry fenrir.

I slowly pushed myself into a sitting position so I could get a thorough view of Vincent. He was still unconscious. It only made me feel marginally better that I could see his chest rise and fall. I wanted to go to him, but Darby flashed me an expression that said I'd get slapped down hard if I dared.

The stillness around us grew more oppressive. As the agonizing minutes ticked by, I realized I needed the fox dryant to get us out of this alive. I searched my pithways for any sign of an internal spark. When that didn't work, I mentally reached out to the possible storm forming above us. Was it just the weather or the fox? Or me? The gathering breeze filled me with soothing air pith, but other than that, didn't offer any answers.

A sudden rustling of leaves had us all facing that direction, fingers twitching to draw sigils. Instead of a wolf vaettur, though, a black-tailed doe treaded timidly out of the woods. She sniffed the air with her wet nose, ears twitching as she stared at Sertalis.

Darby lifted her hand to her mouth. "One of Tabitha's kidama."

Sertalis growled at her. "Shoo. Go away. This place is dangerous."

To my surprise, the doe did take a soft step backward. Everyone visibly relaxed as she retreated into the trees.

Until more soft swishing sounds rose in a chorus around us.

Like synchronized swimmers, an entire herd of black-tailed deer of all ages, genders, and sizes crawled out of the forest. They surrounded us in a near perfect circle on both sides of the stream bank. Like the doe before, they sniffed the air and focused their intense black eyes on Sertalis, a few even pawing the dirt and crying out.

We'd been mobbed by Tabitha's kidama.

Tears streaked down Darby's face. "They know Tabitha's in the lesion. They can sense her."

"Utter nonsense," Sertalis huffed into his moustache, clearly unnerved by the unblinking stares of so many deer.

Darby's tears intensified. "I thought you believed me when I told you I sensed Tabitha in the magma!"

"Grief makes people imagine strange things," Sertalis said.

Of course he'd minimize actual facts. "I believe you, Darby. And so does Guntram and the Oracle."

"Shut up!" she yelled at me. Then she turned back to Sertalis. "We have to abort the plan."

"What?" Sertalis snapped. "Why?"

"Tabitha's kidama are in danger. The fenrir will slaughter them."

"They'll be fine. I'm here to protect them."

I laughed with no mirth. "Because that worked out so well before."

Darby shifted the ground underneath me so fast, my thighs were submerged before I could do anything about it. "Stay out of this, Ina, or so help me—"

The fenrir popped out of nowhere, directly in front of the first doe that had entered the clearing.

The doe didn't even have time to scream. I honestly don't know if she understood how she died. One second we were arguing, and the next, the massive fenrir (had it grown a few feet since our last encounter?) had its jaws around her throat. Her body whiplashed as she became limp, then both she and the fenrir disappeared from view.

All this happened, and not a single one of us had moved an inch to stop it.

The other black-tailed deer screeched in terror,

although they didn't try to flee back into the forest. A stunned Sertalis sent a belated fireball in the fenrir's general direction, but all it did was illuminate a shadowy section of forest before dying with a deflated sizzle.

We were so screwed. Even with lightning, I wouldn't have been able to stop the fenrir.

But I couldn't just stand there helpless either. "Throw me the lightning charm!" I yelled at a stunned Darby. "It may have some juice left in it!"

To my surprise, Darby actually put my necklace in her fist and pulled her arm back.

Sertalis's face twisted into an ugly scowl. "Don't you dare! She'll kill us all!"

"You're the one who's going to get us killed, all just to soothe your butthurt ego!" I tried Darby one last time. "Use your brain, Darbs! The fenrir could slaughter everyone here, including the deer. We need every last bit of our collective magic to survive."

But Sertalis had convinced her. Darby lowered her arm.

I'd had it with both of them. If they stood between Vincent and me walking out of this alive, I'd fight them both, handicapped or not. I drew squares within squares to release me from the earth, then gathered as much ambient pith into myself as I could.

Before I could act, a low growl emitted from somewhere in the foliage around us, impossible to pinpoint its origin. The deer pranced on their hooves while we whipped our heads around. I searched desperately inside myself for the fox dryant, but I could only identify the four elements flowing inside me.

Vincent broke the tension first, moaning as he emerged from his blackout with slow, blinking eyes. This distracted everyone as we twisted to check out the noise.

The fenrir took advantage of the diversion to pounce on Sertalis.

I've never seen such a swift attack, and I hope never to see it again. Sertalis went from looking like a wise mage in his pristine tunic to flailing under a flurry of fangs, claws, and blue swirling lights. The fenrir bit through his defensive charm as if it were paper. Dark blood slashed everywhere, a terrible brushstroke against the fenrir's light-colored fur. The horrified screams haunt my dreams to this day.

But I will give this one thing to Sertalis. As grossly outmatched as he was, he managed to shove a fireball the size of a bowling ball into the fenrir's face. Heat washed over me even at a distance, leaving behind the putrid smell of burnt animal flesh. The fenrir snarled and broke its hold, crashing into the amp ward and busting it open so that its glowing pieces thankfully dimmed to nothing. The wolf howled, then vanished without a trace.

Darby whimpered, fumbling toward the augur, who promptly passed out.

I took a few steps to do the same but noticed a young buck get tossed into the trees not far away. The briefest flash of blue told me the fenrir was far from done with us.

"It's picking off the deer!" I shouted. "Darby! GIVE ME MY CHARM!"

This time, my lightning charm flew from her fingertips. I grabbed it, identifying a familiar pinprick of lightning pith still contained within. Not much but better than nothing. I absorbed it quickly into my pithways, fingers itching to banish this bastard.

It's hard to describe how your mind stops when confronted with such a quick, multi-pronged attack. Three more deer were struck down near the trees. I kept jerking my attention between Sertalis and the latest fallen deer, waiting, watching. Seconds ticked by like hours. I heard Darby whisper soothing things to a groaning Sertalis, but I blocked her out. I had to anticipate the next attack.

Then my chance came. The fenrir reappeared in front of a fawn to my right. I let go of my locked 'n' loaded lightning pith with a five-pointed star. I thought I'd hit my target.

But I didn't. The fenrir blinked out of existence before the lightning struck. It grazed the screeching fawn, instead, who stumbled to the ground next to his mother.

"Dammit!" I would never be fast enough, not if the fenrir could teleport that quickly. And now I was completely out of lightning pith.

Vincent pushed himself up by the arms, his bleary expression raking over the chaotic scene. "Ina? What's going—"

The fenrir pounced right on top of him.

I involuntarily let out a high-pitched wail of pure terror, agony, and despair all rolled into one. I was completely useless as the fenrir aimed its sharp teeth straight at Vincent's throat. Vincent tried to twist out of its hold, but he was trapped. I waited for the gore to follow, unable to tear my gaze away even if it meant seeing him get eviscerated right before me.

But at the absolute last second, the fenrir jerked backward, dazed. Snarling, it went for another sharp bite. It mouthed an invisible bubble that it couldn't penetrate to access its victim. It tried to rake its claws over Vincent, but its paw smacked into something two inches before it could do any damage.

Oduvan's defensive charm was working. It wouldn't last forever, but it at least bought me precious time.

I searched around my pithways for lightning, and when that failed, any element. Instead, something else churned deep inside me, in a corner of myself I didn't know existed. A growing fury, rising in short bursts, clawing to be free.

Let me out.

I faltered. That definitely hadn't been my thought.

The fenrir writhed on top of Vincent. "Help!"

I focused on that foreign sensation, hoping it wouldn't kill me. "You want out? Then come out!"

I was vaguely aware of the gathering storm above me. Thunder crashed and lightning split the dark clouds in two.

But it was nothing compared to the chaos growing inside me. Lightning pith, ten times as powerful as I've ever felt, engulfed my pithways. I couldn't contain it all. Electricity rolled off me as if I'd become a living Tesla coil. One random arc exploded a nearby log into splinters. Another flew toward Darby, who yelped as it grazed her.

She scrambled to the side. "Watch what you're doing!"

Only it wasn't technically me doing it. From that sparking chaos, the fox dryant leaped out of my body, a ghostly apparition that solidified as she landed on the ground. Red coated with a silver breast, she stood as tall as my shoulder. Her jackrabbit ears twitched in rhythm with her double tail as she surveyed the chaos around us.

Darby's face paled to the shade of my electric glow. "How…?"

But I didn't have time to deal with her stupor. The fenrir was jerking over the defensive charm's bubble, snapping jaws inches from Vincent's face.

And then the barrier broke, and the wolf's body slammed straight down onto Vincent, knocking all the air out of him.

The kitsune reacted as fast as her elemental power. Zipping across the distance, she slammed into the fenrir, surrounded by a fierce ball of lightning. She knocked the wolf head over heels with her momentum, and the two of them went tumbling to the side. As they hit the ground, the two snapped and snarled at each other like a pair of angry alley cats, sparks igniting like fireworks from the angry fox. Vincent scrambled backward toward me.

I concentrated all my energy on holding the incredible amount of lightning pith inside me, wanting to blast the fenrir back to Letum, but I couldn't get a clear shot. It would be too easy to hit the fox or explode a nearby trunk. My body shook violently with the mounting pressure, and I worried I might accidentally let it go and kill someone. Sweat pooled down my back, causing ambient electricity to sear my skin.

The fenrir suddenly vanished, deciding not to continue its scuffle with the fox. The fox leaped in three bounds back over to me, eyes blazing and hackles raised. Vincent joined us on unsteady feet. The three of us stood in a rough back-to-back triangle, scouring a third of the forest each for the next attack.

Darby had regained her composure, taking a defensive stance over Sertalis's prone body.

Seconds ticked by. Even the deer trembled into terrified silence.

The fenrir went for another deer, this time the largest buck of the herd. I watched in horror as the fenrir avoided the buck's sharp antlers and went for a quick throat puncture.

Darby was having none of it. "Get back!" she screamed, her voice ringing in the small clearing as she sent up an explosion of dirt that rippled the ground below me yards away. A huge boulder clocked the fenrir in the chin before it could grab hold of the buck, and snarling, it vanished once again.

Whoa. Score one for Darby.

But the fenrir outsmarted us anyway. Instead of slinking off for a rebound, it appeared before the fawn I'd saved (had it only been just minutes earlier?) and yanked it upward by the neck for a quick kill. The kitsune bounded toward the wolf, but it disappeared before she could close the distance. She growled, skidding to a halt near in frustration.

Darby howled.

"You gotta zap that thing," Vincent whispered. "It's our only chance."

Tears stung my eyes, sending electrical sparks into my vision. "I can't. It's too fast."

He grabbed my shoulder and squeezed. "You got this. I know you can."

As is to prove my point, the wolf returned, this time right in front us. Mouth still bloodied from its recent kill, it lunged for me. I froze in sheer terror.

Vincent knocked me aside, taking the full force of the impact.

My knees hit the ground, but I came back up in one fluid motion, blood pounding in rhythm to the lightning in my body. At first, all I could see was the wolf draped over Vincent, its coat spattered with the red streaks of its recent kills.

Vincent would die.

But as time ticked forward, it dawned on me that neither of them—wolf nor man—were moving.

Vincent had yanked his hands upward, fingers curling into the wolf's fur. The fenrir's body had slumped forward, teeth still bared and aiming for Vincent's chest, but caught in a still frame. The muscles in its face twitched as Vincent held on for dear life.

He'd frozen the fenrir with his magic.

"Now... Ina... " he managed.

I slid into a sigil stance on autopilot before I realized what I was about to do. "I don't know if I can aim all this lightning!" I cried. "I might hit you!"

He pierced me with his dark eyes, pleading. "Just do it!"

He was right. We had no choice. The wolf was beginning to jerk at its extremities, clearly fighting Vincent's control.

Vincent was going to die either way. And if Vincent let go of the fenrir, not only would everyone here die, but who knew how many others across the Talol Wilds.

Still, I hesitated. I couldn't risk it. I couldn't kill Vincent.

A red paw pushed gently on my knee. The fox dryant cocked her head at me.

I swallowed a lump in my throat. "I can't."

The fox faced the fenrir, a smirk spreading across her face. She crouched low to the ground, and lightning arced in colorless rainbows across her body. My pithways lurched, seeming to connect with her.

I wasn't alone. We could do this together.

I forced myself to channel all that aching lightning pith toward my outstretched palms. Between crackling electricity, I could just make out the fenrir wriggling ever faster on top of a straining Vincent. I concentrated every fiber of my being on aiming the lightning at the fenrir, keeping it as far away from Vincent as possible.

The fox's dual tails switched in a soothing rhythm. My electricity seemed to slow down to that pace, allowing me more control. The pith still rubbed me raw, but somehow, the kitsune lessened my burden, giving me more control of my unstable element.

My vision narrowed, directed on the bloody fenrir.

The fenrir finally recognized me as a threat. It tried to scurry off Vincent, but the park ranger wouldn't allow it. Vincent's muscles tightened to the snapping point as he increased his magical hold.

If he let up even a little, the fenrir would teleport away.

It was now or never. I lifted my right hand to write a jagged five-pointed star. Then I unleashed everything inside me through that sigil.

Electricity arced from not only my finger, but through all the pores of my right arm, disintegrating my hoodie up to the shoulder. The energy shot out in one fierce bolt that flashed like a shooting star. The blast left a hazy image of the scribbled star on my retinas as it struck the fenrir right between the eyes.

Then the world burst into blinding light.

I stumbled forward in the aftermath. I couldn't see anything but a white haze, but I didn't care. I groped around for any sign of Vincent.

I had to know if Vincent had survived that blast.

I ran into something solid. It slipped past me. It might have been the fox dryant or a young deer, it was so low to the ground.

But then Vincent stood, grabbing onto what was left of

my hoodie. "Ina. It's over. You did it."

I collapsed into his arms, letting blubbery tears fall. I didn't care.

He was safe. I never wanted to let him go again.

EPILOGUE

PEOPLE OFTEN LIKE to look at a situation and criticize how it affects them and only them. But reality is often way more complicated than one person's perspective.

After I banished the fenrir, I wanted Sertalis punished. He'd deliberately disobeyed orders by stealing the amp ward and almost gotten us all killed. Even Darby, his accomplice in stupidity, was angry he'd gotten several of Tabitha's black-tailed kidama deer killed. That's one of the many complicated reasons she dropped her transfer petition and opted to stay with the southern homestead.

But the Oracle did not so much as censure Sertalis. She wouldn't discuss her decision, simply allowing him to heal in peace from his near-fatal wounds at the northern homestead. I heard it took him weeks to get over the fenrir bite.

I fumed over Sertalis's lack of consequences until Guntram rightly pointed out that I'd done similar reckless things in the past, and here I was, still a shepherd of Nasci. I accepted that compassion had to work both ways, and the Oracle had a difficult job maintaining the balance of personalities in the Talol Wilds. It's not the decision I would have made, but I could live with it.

We did win one small victory, though. The Oracle declared Sertalis's and Guntram's duel should go forward while Sertalis was still recovering from his substantial injuries. Knowing he could not possibly fight in his current condition, Sertalis begrudgingly forfeited, granting Guntram an automatic win. The two homesteads would remain separate. I imagined Sertalis stewing in that loss and felt a little better.

On a much happier note, Callum and Sipho finally created a successful damp ward that sealed the lesions permanently. A heavy burden lifted off me knowing Tabitha could finally rest in peace. My mom had no idea that her credit card literally saved the planet. I vowed to pay her back with plumbing job money. And in the meantime, the southern shepherds had proven beyond a shadow of a doubt that they were capable of defending their territory.

That really only left the whole "a kitsune lives inside me" problem. Very few people actually knew about it. I'd half expected Darby to flip her lid after the fenrir fight, but she stuck mostly to herself in the Columbia Basin, avoiding contact with the rest of us. Her anger toward me had cooled into a teenager-sized indifference. Sertalis hadn't witnessed anything in his wounded state, and I seriously doubted the Oracle was going to blab my secret to anyone. That left only Guntram who knew, and he promised to remain discreet as he looked into what it meant for me.

And so, the rest of autumn passed, quiet for a change. I went back to routine defensive sigil duty, occasionally banishing a mild, ordinary vaettur. The other southern shepherds returned to their respective territories, meaning I only ran into Sipho and Callum occasionally finishing the harvest chores. Maybe I should have helped them. Maybe I should have been searching for a lot more answers about my freakish heritage.

But instead, I started teaching Vincent about his ken.

That's how I ended up with him one late October afternoon at a Florence beach. The falling temperatures and relentless chill had driven away even the staunchest beachcombers. Only Ronan joined us. He liked to ride the surf and watch Vincent flail at mastering the most basic sigils.

Vincent's reddened fingers twitched for the hundredth time before he slapped them against his legs. "Forget it, Ina. It's like Guntram told you. I'm different because I wasn't trained at the right age. I can't get this."

"Don't give me that crud," I snapped back. "They all told me I was too old to be a shepherd, and I honed my ken just fine."

"Yeah, but you're the special Japanese shepherd with the live-in fox spirit." He plopped his butt down on the sand, his face tinged with the orange hues of a setting sun. "I'm just a poor schmuck with very limited abilities."

I sat down next to him. "Abilities that saved my life."

He threw his arm around my shoulder, and we huddled together as the salty air washed over us. Ronan grew bored at our romantic inactivity, coming out of the water to bark and wave his antlers at us. Vincent barked back.

I laughed. "See, even Ronan agrees you should keep trying."

He sighed. "I know. It just feels weird. I spent my whole life trying to distance myself from my family's kooky, mystical views. Now I'm on the beach with my nature wizard girlfriend practicing my magical form."

"How is everybody by the way?"

He shot me a concerned look. "My mom still thinks you're the devil, if that's what you're asking. Don't count on her ever changing. You stole her baby boy from the life she had laid out for him. Not that I hadn't already rejected that life, but logic isn't her strong suit."

I shrugged. "She's not the only member of your family. Oscar likes me. And Guntram really does want me to make inroads with you all as innates."

Vincent wrinkled his nose. "That sounds so corny, like we have superpowers or something."

"Stopping monsters in their tracks isn't a superpower?"

He held his chapped hands out to me. "I'd feel a lot better if I could at least lift a little sand, like I've been trying for the last hour."

"It would work better if you allowed me to draw an inner heat sigil on you," I teased, tugging on his heavy leather jacket.

"Yeah, but that's cheating."

"Ah, well. The way your lips are turning blue, you'll have to give up soon anyway."

Something shifted in his eyes that made my pithways burn with a non-elemental fire. "Is there any reason you're so focused on my lips?"

"Because they're frozen?"

But Vincent ignored my lackluster sarcasm and instead drew me into his arms for a long kiss that sparked a lot more than just fire pith.

My relationship with Vincent was far from perfect. Both of us were way too stubborn. We clashed hard when we ended up with opposing opinions. But I also knew, deep in my core, that we'd protect each other. He cared for me, and deep down, I realized a vulnerable, scary truth.

I was falling in love with him.

Before I could fall too far down that rabbit hole, Ronan had decided we'd lip-locked enough. Barking like the overgrown dog he was, the seal flopped over our legs, grinding them into the sand.

"Seriously?" Vincent cried as he futilely attempted to push the blubbery mass off.

Vincent's fingers twitched, and the seal froze stiff under his magic. Vincent shoved him aside, muttering, "At least I'm getting better at that."

Maybe, although Ronan didn't appreciate it much. Once Vincent let go, the dryant charged back into the protesting park ranger. I could only laugh as seal and boyfriend clashed. He'd come a long way for a guy who didn't believe in magic.

THANK YOU FOR READING!

It means so much to me that you've read Ina's story all the way through Book 8! If you'd like to support me as an author, please consider leaving an honest review on Amazon for this series. It not only lets me know you care, but encourages other readers to check out Ina's world. (Also, if there's a big enough fan base to continue this series, I will write more shepherd books. There are a lot more Ina stories I would like to tell if I know people will read them!)

If you like my storytelling style, I have another portal fantasy series that takes a lonely college dropout from her minimum wage carnival job to a whole new magical world:

MAGIC PORTAL

Finally, you can get **two free** *Magic of Nasci* short stories and always know what I'm writing by subscribing to my newsletter at dmfike.com.

ABOUT THE AUTHOR

DM Fike worked in the video game industry for over a decade, starting out as a project manager and eventually becoming a story writer for characters, plots, and missions. Born in Idaho's Magic Valley (you can't make this stuff up), DM Fike lived in Japan teaching English before calling Oregon home. She loves family, fantasy, and food (mostly in that order) and is on the constant look out for new co-op board games to play.

More places to keep in touch:

Website: dmfike.com
Email: dm@dmfike.com
Facebook: facebook.com/DMFikeAuthor
Amazon: amazon.com/author/dmfike
BookBub: bookbub.com/profile/dm-fike
GoodReads: goodreads.com/dmfike
Instagram: instagram.com/dm.fike

LEGEND OF LLENWALD SERIES

"I drive like I color: outside the lines." – Nobody the gremlin

Avalon Benton has nothing: no parents, no money, and no future. Her bland existence unravels when a mysterious knight statue shows up at the Hall of Mirrors at the theme park where she works. A beggar begins stalking her every move, and she has abilities she cannot explain. As Avalon gets pulled toward a secret world where others covet her legendary powers, she must decide whom to trust—an amnesiac fairy, a shapeshifting trickster, or even her former doctor—all of whom may only be exploiting her for their own gain.

BOOK 1: MAGIC PORTAL

BOOK 2: MAGIC CURSE

BOOK 3: MAGIC PROPHECY

MAGIC OF NASCI SERIES

"I do not recommend striking a whale corpse with lightning. You will regret it." – Ina, nature wizard-in-training

Ina is a rookie nature wizard, learning the ropes of elemental magic—fire, air, earth, and water. She can also wield lightning, setting her apart from the other followers of the goddess Nasci. If you like action-packed urban fantasy with just a hint of a slow-burn romance, you'll love reading about Ina's adventures in the Pacific Northwest's national forests.

BOOK 1: CHASING LIGHTNING

BOOK 2: BREATHING WATER

BOOK 3: RUNNING INTO FIRE

BOOK 4: SHATTERING EARTH

BOOK 5: SOARING IN AIR

BOOK 6: RISING SCORN

BOOK 7: GATHERING SWARM

BOOK 8: HOWLING STORM

APPENDIX: NAMES AND TERMS

This section contains a glossary of Nasci-specific terms and characters with pronunciations, presented in alphabetical order.

Afanc (aw-FAHNK): A beaver vaettur with crocodile features.

Augur (AW-ger): The second highest mastery in the shepherd hierarchy. Augurs have complete control over one element, have a special link to their kidama species, and can train eyas-level shepherds.

Azar (uh-ZAHR): A talented fire shepherd.

Banish (BAN-ish): To send a vaettur back to Letum using magical means.

Baot (bout): A water shepherd who spends most of his time in the Pacific Ocean.

Bitai Wilds (bee-TAHY wahylds): The ecological region of desert encompassing the American West and Mexico that is overseen by a specific sect of shepherds.

Boobrie (BOOB-ree): A giant camouflaging bird vaettur.

Bound (bound): To seal a shepherd's pithways so that they can no longer access their magic.

Breach (breech): The interdimensional portal vaetturs create to travel from Letum to our world.

Bundun (BUHN-duhn): A scorpion vaettur.

Callum (KAL-uhm): Forge apprentice for the southern homestead.

Charm (chahrm): An object that stores pith or recreates the properties of a sigil.

Chumal (CHOO-mahl): A locust vaettur that tends to travel in swarms.

Cleft (kleft): An opening in the earth where vitae spills.

Cockatrice (KAH-kuh-tris): A dragon and rooster hybrid vaettur with a Medusa gaze.

Cologat (KOH-loh-gaht): A rat vaettur covered in feathers.

Darby (DAHR-bee): A rookie shepherd with a talent for earth magic.

Dryant (DRAHY-ant): An animal with magical powers that guards others of its kind or territory. A dryant used to be a normal animal until it was blessed with Nasci's essence.

Elif (EY-lif): The forger of the northern Talol Wilds homestead.

Etching (ECH-ing): A symbol that is marked on a specific object to give it pith or the properties of a sigil.

Eyas (AHY-uhs): A rookie (and the lowest level) shepherd.

Fechin (FE-chin): Guntram's favorite raven kidama.

Fenrir (FEN-reer): A legendary wolf vaettur.

Forger (FORJ-er): A follower of Nasci who can sense the four elements (earth, fire, air, and water) and redirect them into objects.

Golem (GOH-luhm): A creature made of pure pith.

Guntram (GOON-trahm): Ina's mentor and master air augur. Ina sometimes calls him Jichan (JEE-chahn), which means "Gramps" in Japanese.

Gyascutus (gee-uh-SKOO-tuhs): A wild boar vaettur with one side of its legs longer than the other to walk on hills.

Haggard (HAG-erd): A derogatory term for a shepherd that began training after puberty.

Homestead (HOHM-sted): A secret base with farms and other resources that shepherds visit to rejuvenate themselves and gather supplies.

Ina (EE-nah): A rookie shepherd with mysterious lightning powers. Her real name is Imogene Nakamori (IM-uh-jeen Nah-KAH-moh-ree).

Jortur (JOR-ter): One of Tabitha's favorite black-tailed deer kidama.

Kam (kam): Sipho's female, dark-coated mountain lion who's active at night.

Kappa (KAHP-pah): An aquatic humanoid frog vaettur.

Kembar stones (KEM-bahr stohns): Two stones that are linked like wisp channels.

Ken (ken): Magical sight granted by Nasci that allows a person to sense pith and see vaetturs and dryants.

Kenawa (ken-AH-wah): A small toad vaettur.

Khalkotauroi (kal-koh-TOU-roi): A fiery bull vaettur.

Kidama (kee-DAH-mah): A species of animals that augurs can communicate with telepathically and give orders to.

Lesion (LEE-zhuhn): A wound in the earth unnaturally inflicted upon Nasci.

Letum (LE-tuhm): The realm where the vaetturs originate.

Mishipeshu (mi-shee-PE-shoo): An aquatic feline vaettur with mysterious powers.

Mulruka (muhl-RUH-kah): A jackal bat vaettur.

Nasci (NAHS-kee): The goddess that lives in the center of the Earth who grants elemental powers to her followers.

Nur (ner): Sipho's male, light-coated mountain lion who's active during the day.

Onyara Wilds (ohn-YAHR-ah wahylds): The ecological region of temperate deciduous forests of the Eastern United States that is overseen by a specific sect of shepherds.

Oracle (OR-uh-kuhl): The highest level of shepherd who leads all shepherds within a Wilds territory.

Petition (puh-TISH-uhn): A grievance raised by a shepherd that must be resolved by the Oracle.

Pith (pith): The essence of fire, earth, air, or water that can be converted into magical energy.

Pithways (PITH-weys): A magical system that shepherds have inside their bodies to redirect and store pith.

Rafe (reyf): A mysterious stranger who shows up in the woods.

Ronan (ROH-nuhn): An antlered harbor seal dryant that lives on the Oregon coast.

Sertalis (SUR-tah-lis): Fire augur for the northern homestead in the Talol Wilds.

Shepherd (SHEP-erd): A follower of Nasci who can store the four elements (earth, fire, air, and water) in their bodies and cast them using sigils. Also the third highest mastery of shepherd, just above an eyas.

Shepherd Trial (SHEP-erd TRAY-uhl): A rite of passage an eyas takes before becoming a full-fledged shepherd.

Sigil (SIJ-il): A symbol drawn in the air by shepherds to convert their pith into a specific magical spell.

Sipho (SI-foh): The forger of the southern Talol Wilds homestead.

Sova (SOH-vah): A northern spotted owl dryant with metallic mauve streaks in her wings.

Tabitha (TAB-i-thuh): Darby's mentor and master earth augur.

Talol Wilds (tah-LOL wahylds): The ecological region of temperate rainforests stretching from British Columbia to northern California that is overseen by a specific sect of shepherds.

Vaettur (VEY-ter): A predatory creature from Letum that enters our world to devour pith via animals and dryants.

Vincent Garcia (VIN-suhnt gahr-SEE-uh): A game warden for the Oregon State Police.

Vitae (VEE-tahy): The lifeblood of Nasci used to create new dryants.

Ward (wawrd): A forge enchantment that either dampens magical energy (damp ward) or amplifies it (amp ward).

Wisp channel (wisp CHAN-el): Glowing lights that shepherds use to teleport large distances.

Wuaro (WAHR-oh): A Bitai Wilds shepherd specializing in water.

Yoi (YOH-ee): The Oracle of the Talol Wilds.

Zibel (ZAHY-bel): A shepherd who spends most of his time in the Oregon Dunes.

A SPECIAL THANK YOU

Writing a book is one thing, getting it out to the world is another. Many talented people gave this book the professional care it deserved. I found my editor Lori Diederich through the 20Booksto50K Facebook group, an invaluable resource for new writers. Sara Smestad modeled for photographer Danan Rolfe so we had plenty of great photos of Ina to choose for the cover.

Sandra Schiller and Jennifer Marshall were fantastic beta readers, catching many pesky grammar errors. Samantha Marshall also provided support during the writing process.

One final shoutout to Jacob Fike, who lends both his time and artistic skills to making each of my books better. I couldn't do this without him.